Ares was taken aback to find a blonde in a long shimmering green dress standing barefoot in the sand only a few feet away, her shoes clutched in one hand. It was, to his astonishment, *the bridesmaid*, who had caught his attention earlier that day.

Why? She was downright stunning, from her sheet of natural blond hair to those bright aqua-green eyes framed in her heart-shaped face with skin so flawless, her complexion glowed.

"Can I help you with something?" he asked politely in English because he was aware that the sole bridesmaid was the bride's sister.

Nervousness made her twitch, and her extraordinary clear eyes evaded his. "I was rather h-hoping I could help you," she stammered in a rush. "If you need a fake wife in a hurry for a price, *I'd* like to put myself forward as a candidate."

And Ares, who was very rarely surprised by any development in life, was totally astounded by that proposition.

Cinderella Sisters for Billionaires

Once upon a time...Cinderella met a billionaire!

There is one thing that the Davison sisters know all too well: life *isn't* a fairy tale! Until their ordinary lives are made extraordinary...by the arrival of two billionaires. But while it feels like the start of two love stories for the ages, will the Cinderella sisters live happily ever after?

Find out in...

Enzo and Skye's story
The Maid Married to the Billionaire

and

Ares and Alana's story
The Maid's Pregnancy Bombshell

Both available now!

Lynne Graham

THE MAID'S PREGNANCY BOMBSHELL

HARLEQUIN®
PRESENTS™

Recycling programs
for this product may
not exist in your area.

ISBN-13: 978-1-335-59302-3

The Maid's Pregnancy Bombshell

Harlequin Enterprises ULC
22 Adelaide St. West, 41st Floor
Toronto, Ontario M5H 4E3, Canada
www.Harlequin.com

Printed in U.S.A.

Lynne Graham was born in Northern Ireland and has been a keen romance reader since her teens. She is very happily married to an understanding husband who has learned to cook since she started to write! Her five children keep her on her toes. She has a very large dog who knocks everything over, a very small terrier who barks a lot and two cats. When time allows, Lynne is a keen gardener.

Books by Lynne Graham

Harlequin Presents

The Italian's Bride Worth Billions
The Baby the Desert King Must Claim

Cinderella Sisters for Billionaires

The Maid Married to the Billionaire

The Stefanos Legacy

Promoted to the Greek's Wife
The Heirs His Housekeeper Carried
The King's Christmas Heir

Visit the Author Profile page
at Harlequin.com for more titles.

CHAPTER ONE

THE GREEK TYCOON Ares Sarris was a billionaire loner. He had shed his team of bodyguards for the occasion of the Durante wedding because they kept everyone at arm's length and he did not like to lend truth to the rumour that he was antisocial... even if he *was*. His unusual silver-blond hair glittered below the lights, his dark eyes very serious, his lean, strong face taut.

He had had a long hard road to the remarkable triumphs that were now his. Born in the back streets of Athens, he was the child of a drug-addicted mother and a rich man, averse to taking responsibility for his blunders. Furthermore, his earliest memory was of his mother calling him a mistake and abandoning him. He didn't look back to those days very often because his childhood had been a nightmare.

Yes, he acknowledged with the grudging aspect of an intellectual man who refused to dwell on the past, his life was very much better now. People didn't tell him what to do any more. They didn't denigrate him or hit him. They didn't act as though his genius level IQ were either some hellish annoying fault or a blessing he didn't deserve. Why? He was much too rich now to be that vulnerable and that made him smile because he had only first set out to make money at the age of eighteen to feel *safe*.

His immense wealth, nonetheless, had failed to protect Ares from being coerced by an old, bitter, snobbish woman he had never met into doing what he didn't want to do. To inherit the Sarris ancestral home as the bastard that he was, he had to be married. *Married!* As desirable a prospect to a male as private and reserved as Ares as sticking his hand into an open fire and the vindictive old witch had known it too! Why else had his grandmother imposed that clause in her will? By law, prevented from leaving the property to anyone other than the last living Sarris, she had contrived to slip in, 'Ares and his wife'.

Katarina Sarris had been well aware that Ares, foolishly frank in the only press interview he had ever given at the age of nineteen, on the acquisition of his first billion, had sworn *never* to marry. Although he had never met the woman who had been his late father's mother, and only a disastrous plane crash killing both his father and his half-brothers in adolescence had finally allowed him to be publicly recognised as a Sarris, Ares longed to possess that firm family foundation of history that had eluded him all his life.

His birth father's denial of his existence when he was a child had broken something in him while also warning him that his bone-deep need for validation was a dangerous weakness. Through DNA tests done at the time, the family lawyers, however, had acknowledged that Ares was a Sarris and had ensured that his educational needs were met. His grandmother, appalled by his background and antecedents as only a very snobbish woman could be, had refused to meet him even after the rest of her family had died. That the sudden death of his father and legitimate half-brothers had immediately given Ares recognition as a Sarris had been a tragic truth. But sadly, no warm welcome had awaited Ares in the bosom of his long-lost family when he'd finally arrived.

Ares had long told himself that he did not need that welcome now that he was an adult. But that house, the home of his paternal ancestry, could not, *should* not be denied to him by some petty clause in a will. Of course, he could have gone to court and easily overturned his grandmother's will but Ares refused to allow his sordid background to be exposed in an open court. As a child and teen-ager, he had undergone deep humiliation on that score. He would never subject himself to that anguish and embarrassment again. No, marrying a stranger simply to meet the exact terms of the will was, by far, the wiser option and a quick, clean solution to a thorny problem.

And that recollection brought Ares straight back to this evening's idiocy. He groaned, pacing restlessly in the well-lit boarded seating area by the side of the hotel's ornamental lake. His future bride, Verena Coleman, very much a paid role-player in his determination to inherit that property, had demanded this private meeting with him. That the woman should *demand* anything set Ares's even white teeth on edge. Until that evening, he had never actually met the lady in the flesh although she would become his wife at the end of the month. His lawyers had dealt with her. She had signed the watertight complex contract and for a very handsome price she would show up at the altar and start acting as his fake wife.

For a split second, Ares thought that he saw an odd shimmer of movement in the darkness below the trees and he spoke in Greek to ask if anyone was there, and then in Italian. After all, he *was* in Italy. Silence rewarded him and he shrugged a shoulder, reckoning that nobody but him was chilling down by the lake unless they were a smoker and, for very good reasons, he would never belong to that tribe.

At last, he heard the sound of feminine heels tap-tapping down the path to the beach and he frowned. Verena had pushed her way into his presence during the wedding reception and thoroughly exasperated him. She was provocatively dressed in a style he viewed as vulgar and everything he disliked in a woman but, for all that, she would still be his wife come the end of the month. She swam into view, all smiles and heaving cleavage on display. She was a curvy brunette from a minor English aristocratic family but if there was a hint of refined blue blood in her it definitely didn't show on the surface. His lawyers had not done well in choosing her.

'Ares!' she carolled, hurrying towards him as if they were friends when they were not even acquaintances. It had been an unpleasant surprise to meet her at the wedding, which he guessed she had only gained entrance to by accompanying the glitzy wedding planner.

'You were directed to address any enquiries to my lawyers,' he reminded her. 'Why would you need to speak to me in person?'

'This is something that only *you* can deal

with,' she announced importantly. 'I'm in a bit of a pickle, I'm afraid. I'm pregnant.'

'Pregnant?' Ares exclaimed in disbelief, and as quickly added, 'That means you've broken our marriage contract—'

'But why should it matter?' Verena demanded angrily. 'It's not as though sex is included in our arrangement. It's not as if you're even planning to share the same house.'

'If I marry you when you're pregnant, the child will be assumed to be mine and that is a legal maze of complication which I have no intention of touching in these circumstances. I do not want your child approaching me in the future believing that I may be his parent. I do not want the squalid rumours that would engulf us all over time either.'

'So, you're asking me to terminate my pregnancy?' Verena assumed.

Ares lifted his proud fair head high. 'I would not dream of making such a request of any woman, nor would I wish such a sacrifice to be made and laid at my door. No, it is much simpler than that: you've broken the contract. Our arrangement is now at an end.'

'You can't do this to me! I was depending on that money!' Verena flashed back at him furiously.

Ares said nothing because he truly had nothing more to say. Verena had after all already received a substantial payment for merely signing the contract.

'But you *need* a wife by the end of the month!' Verena reminded him.

'You are not the only woman who would be willing to enter a marriage of convenience for a price,' Ares retorted with precision.

Verena slung a handful of filthy curse words at him and stalked off. Ares was appalled and he swung away to look out over the moonlit lake. It had been an error not to request a personal meeting with her *before* he signed that contract. His legal reps had certainly not done him proud with her selection, he reflected grimly. She was too ignorant. She might only have been a fake bride-to-be, but naturally he did not want a boorish woman carrying his name or potentially figuring in the media as *his* wife. The binding NDA she had signed would keep her quiet though. He dug out his phone and texted his chief lawyer to warn him that the search was back on for a bride.

As he spun back round, intending to leave, he was taken aback to find a blonde in a long green dress that shimmered standing barefoot in the sand only a few feet away, her shoes clutched in one hand. It was, to his astonishment, the bridesmaid who had caught his attention earlier that day. Why? She was downright stunning from her sheet of natural blonde hair to those bright aqua-green eyes framed in her heart-shaped face with skin so flawless her complexion glowed. He had watched the men queuing up to take her onto the dance floor, all of them desperate to impress her, and he had noticed her seeming indifference to their efforts with detached amusement. Had he thought of approaching her on his own behalf? No…she was far too young for him, barely out of her teens, in his estimation.

'Can I help you with something?' he asked politely in English because he was aware that the sole bridesmaid was the bride's sister.

Nervousness made her twitch, and her extraordinary clear eyes evaded his. 'I was rather h-hoping I could help you,' she stammered in a rush. 'If you need a fake wife in a hurry for a price, *I'd* like to put myself forward as a candidate.'

And Ares, who was very rarely surprised by any development in life, was totally astounded by that proposition. It was a dazzlingly inappropriate offer as well and he rather thought that her new distinctly rich brother-in-law, Lorenzo Durante, would be shocked to the core by a member of his family approaching any wealthy stranger with such an offer.

An hour earlier

Alana had never had as much attention in her life as she received from the men at her sister, Skye's wedding. But once the novelty wore off, she had no interest. She didn't have room for a man in her life when she was too busy working and the reasons *why* she had to work so hard and so endlessly boiled up afresh in her on the dance floor, making her eyes sting with sudden tears.

She was in debt to her eyeballs but that had to remain a giant secret. Yes, her new brother-in-law, Enzo, could have rescued her from her problems in five minutes. After all, Enzo was very generous. He had bought her a car as a bridesmaid's present, even offered to help her return to her art and design course at university. But to request Enzo's help, she would have to lie to her sister and she couldn't imagine Enzo lying to his bride if she told him the truth. Enzo and Skye had a thing about not keeping secrets from each other and Alana was hiding a *huge* secret that she was determined not to share with the big sister she adored.

Skye had idolised their stepfather, Steve Davison. Absolutely idolised the man who had adopted them and whom they both had called Dad. But the older man had been rather more flawed than Skye could ever have suspected. Unbeknownst to their mother and his eldest daughter, Steve had been a gambler and when he had got into trouble with money he had approached Alana for help, knowing that she was the least judgemental person in his family.

Alana had been far too fond of him to refuse to borrow money on his behalf with the loan shark he had taken her to meet. Every week out of his earnings as a taxi driver, Steve had faithfully brought her his payment towards the loan and there hadn't been a single problem. Well, the problem had really only begun when her mother and stepfather were killed in a train derailment the year before and Alana was left struggling to keep paying that loan out of what little she earned as a hotel maid.

But even worse, the debt kept on growing at a fantastic rate. She was paying a phenomenal interest rate and she knew it was illegal but there was nothing anybody could do about that aspect when the loan was in her name and her stepfather had picked a moneylender who was more of a criminal than an upstanding loan officer. Steve Davison had wanted that debt off the books, under the counter, *hidden* and she had made the biggest mistake of her life when she had agreed to the debt being placed in her name.

And when it had occurred to Alana that the best thing she could do with that lovely new car Enzo had bought her would be to sell it for the cash, she had cringed in shame and guilt and had left the wedding reception to seek the darkness down by the lake to lick her wounds. Of course, she couldn't *sell* that gift, but she genuinely didn't have the money to run a car in any case. She got around on a bike for good reasons. Not because she was obsessed with keeping fit, as her sister had teased… oh, if only Skye knew the truth!

But as Alana sank down on a rock in the shadows of the thick belt of trees girding the beach, she knew she wasn't ever going to tell Skye the truth about their stepfather's gambling debts. They had two younger siblings, Brodie and Shona, aged two and one, and Skye had taken full charge of them. She and Enzo were currently in the process of adopting Alana's little brother and sister. Skye had done enough. She had already made more than enough sacrifices on their family's behalf and she *deserved* to retain her illusions about the late father she had adored.

Now it was Alana's turn to do *her* bit and continue to handle the unfortunate financial repercussions of their parents' premature demise. Making heavy weather of her difficulties wasn't going to change anything, she scolded herself impatiently.

As footsteps sounded on the board path above the beach she glanced up, momentarily drawn from her unhappy reverie. A very tall, broad-shouldered male stepped into view below the fairy lights strung round the seating area. Instantaneous recognition leapt through Alana: it was Ares Sarris. That platinum fair hair was unmistakeable, although it had got a little longer since she had first seen him at the Blackthorn Hotel where she worked. He was probably a guest at her sister's wedding, although she hadn't noticed him at the reception because there were hundreds of guests.

The one and only time she had seen Ares Sarris before had been in the Presidential Suite at the Blackthorn Hotel. A US president had stayed there once to play golf and there was a plaque on the wall commemorating his visit. Ares had taken Alana's breath away at first glance. Give him a pair of feathered wings and a sword and he would resemble a warrior archangel. Her cheeks burned in the darkness. What a silly comparison! But, seriously, the guy *was* heartbreakingly beautiful from the crown of his silvery blond head to the soles of his doubtless handmade shoes. He had stopped her in her tracks, made her fumble her words and stare and she still winced thinking about that moment and of how she had later watched him leaping into his helicopter to leave again. She was a grown woman, not an adolescent fangirling over a popstar.

As a female came tripping down the same path, Alana looked on curiously while also beginning to rise to her feet to leave and then the woman announced quite loudly that she was pregnant and Alana dropped back down on her rock perch in shock because she definitely didn't want to walk out into the middle of *that* kind of scene and the only way off the beach would be past the couple. Their voices carried very clearly even though she was trying hard not to listen. The conversation was too confidential to interrupt, she told herself, all the while as her brows rose so high they vanished into her hairline because the idea that Ares Sarris, in all his gorgeous bronzed-angel glory, could have to *pay* a woman to marry him shook her rigid.

By the time, the foul-mouthed lady had departed in a snit, however, Alana's brain was engaged in an entirely different direction. The baby wasn't his? He *needed* a fake wife? He was willing to pay for the service? No sex was involved? In the midst of her frantic ruminations, it struck her that here was a vacancy she could fill, a job with better prospects than the one she had because she knew that Ares Sarris was even richer than her brother-in-law. According to repute, the Greek technology mogul was one of the richest men in the world.

Was she a gold-digger to even think of approaching him?

It was disgusting, wasn't it? To be so desperate for money that she would consider such an option? But that same desperation moved Alana stiffly and uncertainly out of the shadows. What drove her forward was remembering the days she'd lain sleepless, fretting about how she would scrape enough cash together to make the next payment to Maddox, the moneylender. He was a nasty, revolting little man, who had told her more than once that there were *other* options if she was struggling to find the money. She strongly suspected that Maddox was a pimp.

Focusing on a point somewhere to the left of Ares Sarris, after he had asked her whether he could help her with something, she heard herself stammer in a mortifyingly little voice, 'I was rather h-hoping I could help you. If you need a fake wife in a hurry for a price, *I'd* like to put myself forward as a candidate. I'm in debt and I need the money,' she added, like an afterthought.

Ares loosed an unexpected laugh because she was so embarrassed and so gauche and so young that she couldn't even look him in the eye. 'Does Enzo know about this?'

Alana's cheeks flamed and she looked up at him, disconcertingly aware of his great height in comparison to her below average five feet three inches, to say, 'Of course, he doesn't. There are very good reasons why I can't go to Enzo for help.'

Credit-card debt, Ares ruminated, extravagance, drugs? 'If it's drugs, I should be sharing this conversation with him. I'm not a snitch but you are his family now and, in his position, I would want to know such a thing.'

Alana blanched. 'It's not drugs!' she gasped in horror. 'What do you think I am?'

Ares chuckled, amused yet again by her sheer incredulity at such a suggestion. 'I know nothing whatsoever about you. How do I know whether or not you're a party girl?'

'Well, I'm *not*!'

'But you are an eavesdropper,' he pointed out drily.

'I heard the woman say she was pregnant and then I thought I couldn't interrupt because it was too private and I didn't want to embarrass anyone,' she protested vehemently. 'I didn't intend to hear the rest of it. I just felt trapped there in hiding. I'm very sorry that I heard what I shouldn't have.'

'How can you possibly apologise when you're trying to *use* what you heard?' Ares demanded unanswerably.

'If I wasn't pretty desperate, I wouldn't have dreamt of coming up to you like this!' she muttered shakily.

He gazed down at her. The jewelled eyes glistened with tears. A rare shard of compassion infiltrated Ares Sarris, by repute a male with a heart of stone. Yes, he would be asking her to sign an NDA on his behalf in the near future, but she couldn't hide a single emotion that crossed her lovely face. Honesty, innocence and regret shone out of her like a luminous light and he found that weirdly attractive because he was infinitely more accustomed to women who concealed every genuine feeling.

'How old are you?' he enquired.

'Twenty-one,' she told him with a hint of defiance.

She was a little older than he had guessed but not by much. Listening to her, he felt about a century more mature because he didn't believe that he had ever enjoyed such innocence. 'Sit down,' he urged.

'Why?' she asked even as she obediently sat down.

In silence he detached her shoes from her loose grip and crouched athletically low to attach them to her sandy feet. 'I'm assuming you don't want to walk them into the water first?'

Swallowing hard, she shook her head in agreement, seemingly dumbstruck by his assistance with her shoes. He brushed sand away with a light sweep of his hand across the top of her foot and

Alana shivered, extraordinarily conscious of the firm fingers at her ankle holding it steady. Unwarily, she looked up at him for the first time and sank into dark eyes that under the lights above were tortoiseshell perfection set in his lean bronzed face. Every shade of amber and gold swirled in those eyes. And those cheekbones, she enumerated, that sculpted shadowed jaw line, that unexpectedly full sensual mouth and the faint breeze playing with the silvery fair strands across his sleek dark brows. She wanted to *touch* him. In all her life she had never wanted so badly to reach out to touch anyone and she pushed her hands below her thighs to ensure that she kept them to herself.

'You're not even considering me for the job, are you?' Alana condemned. 'You think I'm—'

Ares looked levelly back at her. 'Too young, too naïve and probably unreliable into the bargain.'

'You're only twenty-nine. I read that somewhere!' she added with the speed of embarrassment lest he suspect that she had searched out information about him, which she had many weeks earlier after his stay at the hotel. And in terms of an online search the known facts about Ares Sarris were very few and far between beyond his meteoric success as a tech mogul. Ares certainly didn't live a playboy lifestyle in the public eye as her brother-in-law had done before he'd met her sister. He had been described as reclusive and mysterious because no-body seemed to know how or, indeed, even quite *when* he had appeared in the Sarris family.

'And I'm not unreliable, not the least bit unreliable!' she snapped in fiery addition.

Ares vaulted upright again, amusement his guiding principle in her presence and a rare experience for him. But for all that, he was very much aware that she was a true beauty in that unadorned classic way that so many women sought but missed out on. She sported nothing greater than a hint of shadow on her lids and lip gloss. And as he straightened and caught an accidental glimpse of her full creamy breasts below the neckline of her dress, he went momentarily rigid, fighting off an erection, because, in truth, it was quite some time since he had been with a woman. The reminder that he was a fully adult male with hormonal impulses was unwelcome to Ares. He had always put work first and foremost, scheduling occasional sex into his timetable while simultaneously reminding himself that sex was an indulgence he could do without.

He extended his hand. 'Let me walk you back to the hotel,' he suggested smoothly.

'I would be really good as a pretend wife,' Alana told him earnestly, much as if she were trying to sell herself in an interview.

His handsome mouth quirked. 'Why do you think that?'

'I'd do everything I was asked to do and think myself lucky to get the opportunity,' she continued winningly. 'I'd also hopefully be a bargain in terms of price!'

Above her down-bent head, Ares could not resist a wicked grin. 'Let's hope nobody else overhears *this* particular conversation.'

'I only want enough to settle my one debt,' she continued doggedly.

'And how much is this debt?' Ares could not resist asking, ridiculously diverted by her and not bored the way he usually was with her sex.

'It's a *lot*,' she warned him in an undertone and then she practically whispered, *'Thirty thousand pounds...'*

Ares was trying hard not to laugh out loud. 'Yes, you would be a very inexpensive acquisition for that amount—'

'Are you considering me yet?' she prompted hopefully, pausing on the path as the lights of the big hotel loomed into view ahead of them.

Ares gazed down at her with eyes that were now black as the night sky. 'I'm afraid not. What's your name? I don't even know your name.'

'Alana… Alana Davison. You're not giving me a chance,' she complained.

'Why would I?' Ares asked drily.

'Because it would be perfect for both of us. Obviously, you don't want a proper wife and I certainly don't want a husband!' she pointed out cheerfully. 'And I'm very trustworthy. I promised my dad before he died that I would never tell my sister, Skye, about what he had done and I never have because if I did tell her, it would *hurt* her too much. I also have no family other than Skye and Enzo to be suspicious and, let's face it, like most newly marrieds they'll be very much wrapped up in their own little bubble. I'm a very hard worker—'

'I wouldn't be hiring you to do actual work,' Ares inserted into that animated flood.

'I'm sure I could do something. I'm very willing and adaptable. I like kids and pets...' Alana looked up at him hopefully.

'I have neither to offer for your care,' he divulged ruefully, finding himself strangely reluctant to hurt her feelings when she was trying so hard to impress. 'Is the hard sell over? Could we now return to the hotel?'

Her expressive face reddened as she moved on down the path. 'At least promise to think about it... about me as a possibility,' she pressed.

Ares released his breath on a slow hiss, drew out his phone and opened it. 'Give me your number but, in all likelihood, you *won't* be hearing from me,' he warned her wryly. 'But my lawyers will be asking you to sign a non-disclosure agreement very soon.'

'Of course I'll sign it,' she muttered hurriedly, keen to reassure him.

'I could pay you for doing that—'

'No, no, no!' she exclaimed in dismay. 'You can't pay me for having done something I *shouldn't* have done—surely you see that?'

And that immediate refusal of cash when she was desperate for it was the most eye-opening experience that Ares had had in years. She had a sense of honour and that was rare indeed, he conceded as he strode away. She had connected with him on some level he didn't understand but that didn't mean that he appreciated her appeal. Ares didn't like impulsive promptings or anything out of the norm for him. In fact, it made him immediately suspicious and ill at ease, although, he recalled, he had not felt uncomfortable while in her company. For curiosity value alone, he would have a background check done on Alana Davison and his lawyers would have the NDA signed. There would be no further personal contact. Why the hell would there be?

CHAPTER TWO

Where are you?

THAT WAS THE text from Ares four days after Alana had left Italy.

Alana rolled her eyes as she emptied rubbish from a bin and wheeled her trolley back down the corridor. It was seven in the evening. Alana worked a permanent nightshift and the very wealthy clientele she served on the upper floors of the exclusive hotel often arrived and departed at unconventional times. The Blackthorn Hotel offered twenty-four-seven service to their guests.

UK. Working. Busy.

She texted the triple-word response with pleasure, thinking it served him right when he had blown her off in Italy. Doubtless he wanted that

NDA signed, she reflected ruefully, her punishment for having listened to a private conversation when she should have revealed her presence.

That brief text response made Ares grind his teeth together. She was a hotel maid, not a neurosurgeon. She could have spared him a little more information. Of course, if that was how she wanted to play it, he would respond in exactly the same way. He signalled a PA to get Enzo Durante on the line because he wanted a favour. He would buy the Blackthorn. Game on, he thought without really thinking about what he was doing, a reaction weird enough to Ares's precision-orientated brain to have usually inspired deeper reflection. Only it didn't on this occasion because Ares was in full attack mode like a guided missile taking aim at a target.

Forty-eight hours later, as she began her shift at six in the evening, Alana was cornered by the night manager, Martin. 'Why does the new owner of the hotel want to see you?' he demanded.

'The hotel's been sold?' Alana was ridiculously surprised by that news and, as quickly, she scoffed at her reaction. Had she really thought that Enzo would retain ownership purely because she worked in a lowly capacity there? Naturally, that wouldn't strike her brother-in-law as an important fact. Besides, in response to his offer of financing her return to university, she *had* mentioned searching out a better job as her current ambition. That had been her handy excuse when she was not in a position to admit that she could not afford to stop earning while she had a debt to service.

Her brow furrowed as she mulled over the rest of what the night manager had said. 'Why would he want to see *me*?' she asked.

'Maybe because your rich brother-in-law asked him to check on you or something,' Martin replied cuttingly.

Alana reddened. 'I doubt that.'

She was paying the price for the time off she had been granted for her sister's wedding. Initially it had been refused because the hotel was fully occupied and then an order had come down from the owner of the chain to say that she was to receive *any* leave that she requested and her family connection to Enzo had been exposed. And ever since her return she had been treated with suspicion at work, being viewed either as a potential spy or some little rich girl playing at a low-paid job she didn't really need. Nobody seemed to accept that Enzo's wealth had nothing whatsoever to do with her.

'He's in the Presidential Suite so you had better get up there,' Martin said thinly just as a slender brunette came walking down the corridor with a

winning smile aimed at him, and Alana lost his
attention altogether.

A couple of months earlier, Alana had applied
for the assistant night manager position when it
came up. Enzo hadn't known about it because Skye
hadn't wanted to ask her fiancé for a favour for
her sister. And Alana hadn't got the job she was
qualified to do because married Martin was illic-
itly involved with the equally married colleague
of hers who *had* got the job.

Wondering if the new owner was one of the
men she had met at Skye's wedding and very
much hoping he wasn't, Alana ducked into the
staff cloakroom to check that she was tidy and
wash her hands. Her simple brown overall and
maid's frilly mob cap were brown and uninspir-
ing, her hair braided up beneath, her face bare of
cosmetics. Maybe it was just a case of the new
owner being a friend of Enzo's and wishing to be
polite and acknowledge her, she thought wryly.

She knocked on the door of the Presidential
Suite and it was swiftly opened by a guy in a suit
wearing one of those earpieces that signified that
he was in protection work. Her face tense, Alana
moved deeper into the very large reception area
with its opulent seating and a fireplace blazing
with the logs provided.

A very tall figure clad in a black pinstriped

suit of impossibly well-tailored cut rose from behind the desk in the corner, lean bronzed features
so instantly recognisable, she gasped. 'Alana—'

'*You're* the new owner?' The accusation flew
from Alana's lips in angry disbelief, instant wari-
ness and suspicion flooding her. 'Why on earth
would you buy the hotel where I work? Is that
supposed to be some nasty, aggressive threatening
move? *Why?* I agreed to sign an NDA, didn't I?'

Utterly taken aback by that verbal assault, Ares
strode round the desk and right over to her. 'Nasty?
Aggressive? *Threatening?* Of course not, not in
any way,' he assured her with taut emphasis, his
startlingly handsome face reflecting distaste at the
very suggestion.

'Well, it looks like a dodgy move after the
conversation we had on the beach last weekend,'
Alana told him roundly, noting how very tall he
was again. 'It's intimidating.'

'My apologies. That was not my intention,' Ares
lied, and he *knew* he was lying but he still didn't
understand why he had bought the wretched hotel
in the first place and now had nothing more to say
on the subject. It was a good investment, that was
all, he reasoned inwardly.

'So, where's the document for me to sign?'
Alana prompted. 'I need to get back to work.'

Unaccustomed to such a summary dismissal,

Ares breathed in deep, wondering how their meeting could have travelled in such a disconcerting
direction. Like a grenade thrown into a room, she
had exploded his every expectation because he
had vaguely pictured her greeting him with smiles
and warmth. 'I wish to discuss the debt you told
me about—'

Alana tilted her chin, green eyes like emerald
fire throwing defiance. 'That's nothing to do with
you—'

'You have no debts to your name. I had a background check done on you,' Ares revealed with
calm assurance.

Her delicate brows shot high, her slender frame
growing even more rigid. 'And why would you do
something nosy like that?' Alana demanded. 'My
background is none of your business!'

'When you asked me to marry you, you neglected to mention how belligerent you could be,'
Ares breathed with icy restraint.

'Well, now you can be grateful that you're not
suffering a bad case of buyer's remorse!' Alana
shot back at him quick as a flash.

'Miss Davison?' another voice unexpectedly interposed into the seething silence that had fallen
after that response. 'Why don't you come this way
and we'll get the document signed without further ado?'

In shock that there was another human being present, because she had assumed that she was alone with Ares, Alana glanced across the room to see an older man standing in the open archway that led through to the dining area and she turned the colour of an over-ripe tomato in embarrassment. She had contrived to have an argument with Ares Sarris, and she honestly didn't know how that had happened. His unforewarned appearance as the new owner of her place of employment had set off every alarm bell she possessed and only now did it occur to her that she might have overreacted, and she regretted the hot, quick temper that her sister had once told her she should always control.

Her newly guilty mood at having humiliated herself was not improved by walking through that archway to find another two men already seated at the polished table. Both of them studied her as though an alien creature had joined them without warning. Doubtless they had heard every accusing word she had flung at Ares.

Ares disconcerted her even more by stepping past her to politely tug out a chair for her and she sank into it like a stone dropped from a height. 'We'll have some supper after this,' he murmured smoothly as if the previous five minutes hadn't happened.

Her ears almost shot out in incredulity at that

announcement. *Supper?* She thought of the excuse
of working again and shelved it because he *was*
the boss and how had she forgotten that for even
five minutes? Was she totally stupid around Ares
Sarris? The NDA agreement was explained to her
at great and very boring length. Ares sat across
the table from her, probably afraid of her accusing him of intimidation again if he even sat beside
her, she reflected with an inner wince of shame.

In any case, Ares was still showcased in her
mind by the first glimpse she had caught of him as
she'd walked through the door: her warrior angel,
lean, strong face gorgeous but cool and composed
as ice, not even a twitch of a smile anywhere near
his wide mobile mouth. She hadn't seen the tiniest
hint of welcome or friendliness in that image and
maybe she had reacted accordingly because wasn't
she entitled to expect him to have been a little less
frozen after their frank discussion in Italy? Or was
it simply the truth that that reckless and spontane-
ous dialogue by the lake had merely increased his
frozen aspect by a factor of ten?

Afterwards, she had barely been able to believe
the foolish things she had said to him. What an
idiot she had been to corner so sophisticated and
wealthy a man with her stupid irresponsible idea!
Of course, he had said no! She had probably struck

him as being not just a little off the wall but a touch unhinged.

Alana scanned through the document as fast as she could without her reading spectacles while one of the lawyers present offered to take her into the other room to discuss anything she didn't understand. 'That's unnecessary,' she parried, thinking that it took an awful lot of words to warn her that she was never to talk about Ares, write about him or his business or make use of any photographs of him.

As Alana rose upright, Ares stood up as well. 'Let's relax now…'

Alana shot him a look of visible wonderment at that suggestion and Ares almost physically etched a one-up symbol in the air between them. He was relieved, in fact, that she had shown him that she was not fault free. A quick temper and a habit of expecting the worst from people were bearable flaws, although it was not as though he would be spending much time with her, he reminded himself, frowning at the random weird thoughts that infiltrated his very orderly brain in her vicinity.

'Take a seat,' he invited as the legal team filtered out of the suite.

Alana settled down into the sort of sofa that almost swallowed her alive because it was soft and comfortable. The lights dimmed a little and the fire crackled in the grate. 'Isn't this cosy?' she muttered uncomfortably.

'Is that sarcasm?'

'No. I was just thinking that this is much better than vacuuming. But I don't blame you for being wary,' Alana acknowledged, finally looking up to focus on him where he sat opposite. 'I kind of lost the plot earlier. I wasn't expecting to see you ever again. I thought you'd send the NDA in the post...or something.'

'You've seen me at this hotel before, haven't you?' Ares prompted.

Alana nodded. 'I delivered your coffee one night when you were working late. I'm not expecting you to remember me. Guests don't really look at staff in uniform or remember faces.'

Ares said nothing. He didn't remember her. But he imagined a certain type of male would notice her even with her hair hidden. Her shapely legs, her slender yet curvy figure, the vivacity of her green eyes, the flawless skin. The sleazy ones would notice her, he reckoned. 'It's rather an old-fashioned uniform,' he remarked.

'Suits the antique style of the hotel and at least they didn't model it on a French maid's outfit.' She laughed as a knock sounded on the door.

Without any prompting, Alana jumped up and

went to answer it. Tom, one of the young waiters, wheeled in a trolley and grinned at her.

'Sit down, Alana,' Ares instructed.

Talk about the habit of command, Alana thought ruefully, wondering why he would insist on having supper with her. Just to be friendly because of the Enzo connection? Or was there something else? It occurred to her that Ares was as naturally friendly as barbed wire.

'I would still prefer to settle that debt for you,' Ares informed her loftily. 'You have signed the NDA. You could have made a lot of money selling the story of my intended fake marriage to some tabloid newspaper and I am very grateful that you didn't.'

'Because I'm poor and in debt, I can't be expected to behave decently?' Alana quipped. 'I still have standards, Ares.'

'You've had time to think now. Will you…?'

Alana jumped upright with a bright and determined smile. 'Coffee or tea?' she asked, stationed by the trolley.

'Coffee…but—'

'I don't want you offering me money again when I didn't do anything for you. I did what I *should* have done,' she pointed out. 'Don't embarrass me.'

Unfamiliar with interruption and anyone guessing his intentions before he even expressed them, Ares released his breath in a hiss. 'You frustrate me. You are very stubborn. At least tell me what this mysterious debt is.'

Alana breathed in deep and reckoned that there was no harm in clarifying the situation on that score. 'My stepfather was a gambler. Backroom illegal card games, as far as I was able to work out. When he got into trouble with money, he came to me for help,' Alana explained. 'He was deeply ashamed of the gambling, and he couldn't bring himself to confess to my mother or my older sister. I think he was terrified that Mum would leave him over it…he loved her *that* much—'

'But not as much as he loved gambling,' Ares interposed cynically. 'If he'd loved her as much as you think he did, he would have got professional help with his addiction and come clean.'

'In an ideal world,' Alana agreed. 'But he was a weak man, Ares. I'm strong, and my mother was and my sister is, but he *wasn't*. It's a shame because our stepfather was a kind and loving man. In every other field, he was pretty perfect as a dad.'

While she talked, Alana acted like a maid serving him, offering him snacks from the containers on the trolley, furnishing him with a napkin and a plate, pouring his coffee exactly as he liked. And it thoroughly irritated Ares. He didn't like her waiting on him in that demeaning way. He didn't like seeing her in a maid's uniform either. He supposed it was because he felt sorry for her, an unbusiness-like, impractical sensation that was incredibly new to him, but then nobody had ever told him that he should have no feelings whatsoever. Even though he usually did not have.

'How did you get involved with your stepfather's gambling debts?'

'He asked me to take out the loan in my name with the moneylender so that it couldn't come back to him and expose his secret,' Alana explained.

Ares was so outraged by that casual explanation that he clenched his teeth together, sooner than risk saying something offensive, but he couldn't hold it back. 'He was your adoptive father. It was his duty to *protect you*. Instead he took you to a moneylender and bulldozed you into signing up. Is it an illegal loan?'

'I assume it is. But I don't want you thinking badly of Dad. He brought me the money to pay that loan every week for over a year before he died,' she countered. 'He would never have left me to cope with it alone.'

Ares studied her with hungry intensity. Even in a maid's uniform, he found her appealing. Did that mean that *he* was a sleaze? In haste, he averted his attention from her but the vision of her face and curvy little body went with him. What was wrong with him? The heaviness at his groin told him that he was getting hard *again*. It was the originality of her, he told himself. She was like no woman he had ever met before and naturally novelty was a draw. For once, he wasn't bored. He couldn't second-guess her responses. She didn't fish for compliments or talk endlessly about herself and her accomplishments in an effort to impress. But why was he even thinking in such a manner about her?

He had come in person to the Blackthorn because he had wanted to see her again. *Needed* to see her again, no matter how odd that key instinct still seemed to him. For the first time in his life he couldn't fathom what was happening inside his own head and it was driving him crazy. It had to be sex, *lust*, he assumed, compressing his lips on the shocking suspicion that such a base prompting could control him to such an extent. Characteristically, he was appalled by the idea.

'I understand,' he remarked on her defence of her father.

'And I hope you also understand now that you don't owe me anything whatsoever for signing that NDA,' Alana pressed, her green eyes welded to his bronzed features while she tried feverishly hard to fight off her fascination. But he was *so*…together, she selected distractedly. Controlled, contained, impregnable, she sensed, the core of him locked behind high walls. She was all on the surface, nothing concealed or, certainly, very little and he was her total opposite, not a shred of emotion displayed on that lean, darkly handsome face of his.

'I get that that is what you want me to feel but I don't agree with your outlook,' Ares admitted tautly.

'I don't suppose you do, because you're used to putting a price on everything and I suppose people expect to enrich themselves at your expense.'

'That's an odd remark to make when you're the woman who offered to marry me for a price.'

'I'm in a bind, Ares. While I have to service that debt I can't get on with my life or do anything that I want to do.'

'And what do you want to do? Assuming you had a choice.'

Ares watched her emerald-bright eyes cloud in contemplation. 'Return to your university studies?'

'I didn't like my course much. I signed up for it because I wanted a marketable job when I finished because of the loans I took out to finance it,' she admitted. 'I'd probably most enjoy something arty, possibly painting, although I'm not particularly talented as an artist.'

Ares was impressed that she could admit that.

He pictured her painting in one of his houses. He himself did not have an artistic bone in his body but he collected art that he enjoyed for more than its investment value. He liked her utterly un- ashamed honesty, her unexpected standards, her confidence even though she was sitting in front of him in a maid's uniform. He knew Edwin Graves, his suave chief lawyer, would turn white over- night at what he was about to do but, for once, he didn't care about the formalities. He would take a risk on Alana Davison and, although he had only briefly discussed the idea with his lawyers, who had expressed reservations, he knew that *he* had already made up his mind and for that reason he had instructed his lawyer to bring the marriage contract with him for him to look over.

'I'm offering you that job you said you wanted,' Ares intoned. 'That's why I had the background check done.'

Her green eyes widened, and her soft pink lips parted in surprise. 'Oh, well…er…what does it en- tail?'

'We go through a legal ceremony, because I need a wife for legal reasons,' Ares advanced. 'It will last from a few months to, at most, a year. The signing of a contract will be required. If you break the terms included it will be punitive, I warn you. For the period of time that you are pretending to be my wife, you will conduct yourself as though you truly *are* my wife and will engage in nothing that could cause me embarrassment. You will dress well and behave well and that is pretty much it.'

'And I don't even have to live with you?' Alana checked anxiously.

'No. I like my privacy but, for the sake of appearances, I will occasionally visit whichever property you are using.'

'OK. I'm signed up,' Alana told him with a huge inhalation of sheer relief at the very idea of finally being free of the debt that haunted her every waking hour.

Ares frowned, black brows pleating. 'Are you always this impulsive?'

'Don't say it like it's a fault.'

'I see it as such.'

'Do you ever let loose and relax? Because after meeting you twice, I have to wonder.'

'We will have a businesslike arrangement,' Ares countered levelly. 'We will not have conversations like this. Indeed, you will hardly see me for the duration of the contract.'

Alana lowered her hopelessly disappointed gaze and swallowed hard.

'Being attracted to me is unlikely to be a plus in this scenario,' Ares warned her quietly.

Alana's head came up again in a rush. 'I'm not attracted to you!' she snapped.

Ares was almost pleased to discover that some things she would lie about, if cornered. But he was attracted to her too, although he would not have admitted it either, he conceded absently. 'I spoke merely because I don't want any misapprehensions arising between us. There will be no intimacy of any kind.'

'Not a problem,' Alana replied with insouciance.

Ares experienced an extraordinary desire to simply lift her into his arms and show her how much of a problem that hunger could be, but he was too disciplined to succumb to such an urge. 'The contract is on the desk. When you've read and digested it, I'll recall my legal team to act as witnesses.'

'I don't need to read it—'

Dark eyes as sharp as ice picks landed on her. 'You *will* read it from start to finish.'

Alana watched him vault upright with that smooth easy grace that she found so noticeable in his every movement, as if his limbs and his muscles were composed of stretchy silk. He swept a document off the desk and strode back to her extending it and she reckoned that she would not miss his bossy presence in whichever property of his she ended up living in. The fat document was at least a hundred pages long and she looked at him in wonder as she glanced through it.

'You shouldn't punish me just because the last candidate was stupid.' She sighed, beginning very slowly to leaf through, peering at the small print. 'I can't read this without my specs.'

'You read the NDA,' he reminded her.

'As well as I needed to,' she qualified.

'Go and get your spectacles,' Ares instructed impatiently.

Alana got up, which took effort when the squashy cushioning of the sofa wanted to hold her back. 'Gosh, is this what happens when you get rich...you want everything signed, sealed, and delivered like...yesterday?' she commented.

'It is,' Ares responded without apology.

Alana heaved a long-suffering sigh but inside she was crowing in heady delight. She was about to get rid of her stepfather's debt, she was going to get her life and her freedom back! She could hardly believe the sheer joy of release that was flooding through her veins.

Ares watched her bounce out of the room and he smiled. She was pleased. She was happy. Strangely that knowledge satisfied something in him. He assumed it was relief from being at the end of the bride hunt again.

His chief lawyer had intimated some doubts on the score of Alana being the right choice. He had produced exactly the same objections that Ares himself had cherished on first meeting Alana. But some stubborn trait inside Ares had refused to give ground to those sensible doubts. He *liked* Alana and he trusted her. It really was that simple. Her silence in recent days, when she could have spilled what she had overheard to the press and made herself a fortune, had been the conclusive proof he needed that Alana was the absolute right choice.

Alana raced back to the Presidential Suite, her glasses firmly anchored on her nose. She used her key to gain entry, saw no sign of Ares and walked into the dining area to sit down at the table and immediately read the contract. She could have done with a dictionary to interpret some of the words but glossed over those phrases regardless.

'Any questions?' Ares enquired from behind her.

'Yes, what does that word mean?' she asked, pointing a finger.

Ares leant down close to her to look over her shoulder and explained, silvery hair brushing her cheek. He smelled *divine*. Some sort of cologne mixed with warm, clean, male earthiness. Her nostrils flared on the scent of him, her body warming without her volition, her nipples tightening into hard little buds, her legs quivering and pressing close together. Only chemistry, she told herself squarely, nothing to feel bad about. Or at least, she conceded, she wouldn't have felt bad had a guy ever affected her that way before, only no one had until now. Ares Sarris was like a hidden patch of black ice on a road. She needed to learn avoidance techniques. Or did she? Hadn't he said that they would barely see each other?

'My lawyers are joining us to witness the signing,' Ares informed her. 'You'll leave this job in the hotel today.'

'I can't just—'

'If you want this contract, you will. How many people would credit that I've married a maid?' he sliced back at her. 'And I want the details of the debt so that it can be dealt with.'

'Maddox operates out of the back room of the pool hall in town. That's all you need to know. Give me the money and *I* will settle it—'

'No,' Ares said succinctly. 'You will not return to the moneylender in person. It could be dangerous. That is not negotiable.'

'There isn't very much negotiable with you,' Alana dared to say. 'But then you're paying for this, so I suppose that's how it should be, but I can't see what you're getting out of it.'

Ares's innate reserve prevented him from telling her. He would gain immediate ownership of the house he had never once entered as a boy or young man. He would see the portraits of the Sarris family as their last descendant and the name would die out after him because he wasn't planning on providing the next generation. He would pass on single, childless and without fanfare and leave the medieval ancestral estate to the state to use as a tourist attraction.

'All the same, I enjoy a mystery,' she said lightly, turning another page. 'Where will I be living?'

'I haven't decided yet.'

'Well, if you could make your mind up now I could tell Enzo and Skye that you've hired me as a housekeeper for it.'

'A lie of that nature won't work, not when you'll have staff of your own looking after you and calling you Mrs Sarris. Tell your family that we fell in love at first sight and when it doesn't last very long, nobody will be too surprised,' Ares disconcerted her by suggesting with a cynical twist of his lips as though the very idea of love at first sight was preposterous.

'But then they'll expect a proper wedding and I assume you're not planning on that.'

'I'm planning a quick civil ceremony—'

'So how do I explain that when I'm a fairy-tale-bride kind of girl?'

'You tell them that Ares doesn't do parties or celebrations.'

'But that makes you sound really dull, serious and selfish—'

'I am,' Ares slotted in without hesitation.

Alana tilted her head back and looked up at him awkwardly. 'You don't look or act dull.'

Ares shrugged a broad shoulder, unconcerned by her opinion. Certainly, he wasn't a fun guy, a prankster or a party animal or even a womaniser. He was a workaholic. His only other interest was working out in the gym and that was only sensible to maintain good health.

'You'll need to be ready to leave in the morning,' he informed her. 'So, pack tonight.'

'Tonight?' She gasped. 'Where am I going?'

'London to facilitate the rest of the arrangements. I have accommodation ready there for your arrival.'

Alana winced. 'I didn't realise everything would be happening so soon. Saying we fell in love at first sight is not likely to work when I only met you first at the wedding—'

'You say you met me several times here while you were working.'

'Guests don't *meet* chambermaids.'

'You *did*. Let your sister think what she wants of that. It scarcely matters in the scheme of things.

We won't be married for very long,' he pointed out carelessly.

Alana compressed her lips and said nothing. She had to adapt to the truth that, for the next few months at least, her life would no longer be her own to direct. 'Can't I tell Enzo and Skye the truth?'

'I thought you read that contract. You tell a single living soul and you're in breach of contract,' Ares reminded her.

CHAPTER THREE

'YOU CAN'T JUMP into marriage with some guy you hardly know!' Skye fired at her younger sister in incredulous disbelief later that same evening.

'I've clarified everything as best I can but I'm an adult,' Alana forced herself to proclaim even while she had every sympathy for her sister's feelings on having to listen to such unlikely fabrications as Alana had been forced to tell. 'Nobody can stop me marrying Ares and I'm leaving with him in the morning. I won't risk losing him.'

Her sister's husband, Enzo, studied her anxious face with penetrating force. 'He made you sign something to keep you quiet. That's why you can't explain, isn't it?'

Stunned by that accurate reading of the situation, Alana paled and then, overwhelmed by relief by his grasp of the situation, she nodded confirmation in haste.

'What on earth are you talking about?' Skye demanded.

'We're getting fairy stories because she *can't* talk,' Enzo guessed. 'Ares Sarris is notorious for having legal eagles who fire off more non-disclosure agreements than a celebrity's lawyers do. He's a very private individual. I would surmise that Alana is entering a marriage with him because he requires a wife for some business purpose?'

Wearily, Alana nodded again and then just dropped her head, not knowing whether to be pleased or aghast at the impressive level of Enzo's shrewdness. But at that mention of the lawyers' use of NDAs on Ares's behalf, she was suddenly worried that she might have leapt from the frying pan into the fire. Had she been too impulsive? After all, in much the same fashion she had signed that loan agreement in haste and nothing good had come of that decision.

'Does this have anything to do with his sudden desire to buy the hotel from me?' Enzo queried.

'It could do. I'm not really sure,' Alana admitted.

Skye heaved in an audible breath and perceptibly relaxed. 'But what I don't understand is *why* Alana would agree to such a thing when she could come to you for any financial help she might need. Do you know what you're doing right now?'

'Yes, as far as I can establish stuff,' Alana reasoned carefully.

'Is he a trustworthy guy?' she asked her sister, with a nudge of her shoulder to make her younger sibling look directly at her again.

'Very much so,' Alana declared, perspiration marking her short upper lip now that the worst was over and the act of sharing that marital announcement was achieved.

'And obviously you're attracted to him—'

'Obviously.'

'With Ares, you're talking about the ultimate serious, steady male,' Enzo commented in a clear effort to soothe his wife's concerns. 'Never a hint of a scandal about him, definitely *not* a Casanova with women—'

'Well, if he protects his privacy with NDAs there wouldn't be,' Skye chimed in, less impressed than Alana had hoped she would be by that accolade.

'I like him, I respect him and I trust him,' Alana heard herself say in a sudden rush. 'But you can't ever tell anyone that I said that about him!'

And her tiny sister, several inches below Alana in height, burst out laughing at that admission.

'OK, kid sister. I'll trust you to know what's best for you this *one* time, but the moment you doubt this decision or need help, we're here for you,' Skye proclaimed, gathering Alana into a warm, reassuring hug, and all Alana's fears that she might damage her ties to her family by marrying Ares drained away at that same moment.

The next morning, Ares glanced at Alana's delicate profile in the helicopter, noting the tense set of her soft pink lips and edgily recognising her nervous tension. She had signed the contract. Everything was organised, nothing left to go wrong. But any woman could get cold feet about marrying, couldn't she? Furthermore, plans made for his original bride candidate, Verena Coleman, were not a good fit for Alana Davison. At least, in Ares's opinion, if not in his legal team's opinion. They had seemed almost bewildered by his attitude when he'd pointed out the many differences.

How could he possibly dump Alana in an unfamiliar city, expect her to buy a suitable wardrobe for herself and live alone in an apartment? Had she ever lived alone? Thanks to that background check, he knew that she had not. He didn't think her time spent as a maid living in hotel accommodation worth considering. Leaving Alana without family in London would be like dumping one of the babes in wood straight into the witch's cottage, he reflected with deep unease. His chief lawyer, Edwin, might believe that it was acceptable to treat Alana the same way as Verena, but Ares saw such assumptions as belonging under the heading of 'expecting too much'. Alana was years younger, less experienced, less confident, less an awful lot of things, he framed in his own quick and clever brain.

Naturally there would be *some* drawbacks to his choice of Alana as a fake wife and this was one of them. He would need to make more allowances until they reached the married phase and he let her sink or swim on her own. For now, he had to be supportive to ensure the success of their pretence *after* their marriage, he reasoned, and he relaxed at that conviction because that made perfect good sense to him. That also fully explained to his own satisfaction why he had been stressing out—something he *never* did—about leaving her and returning to his usual routine.

'We're going shopping…*together*?' Alana surveyed Ares in astonishment as they walked at a fast rate of knots through the London airport, shielded on all sides by his security team. 'But I thought we weren't going to do *anything* together—'

'Do you know what kind of clothes you need to choose? Do you even know what wealthy women wear at formal occasions?'

Alana winced. 'Well, no, but—'

'That's why you need my assistance,' Ares decreed calmly, satisfied that all his concerns during the flight were now proven.

'But why would I need clothes for formal occasions when you're not planning to take me out anywhere with you?' Alana asked in a hesitant tone, because she had already discovered that Ares seemed to have a definitive answer for absolutely every question.

'There's a benefit in Athens being held by my charitable foundation in a couple of months. I have decided that for the purpose of authenticity we should make at least one public appearance together.'

'I understand,' Alana declared although, in truth, she didn't. What she had originally understood was that Ares was planning to leave her in some city apartment where she was to concentrate on kitting herself out as a credible Sarris bride at his expense. It was true though that she wouldn't have had a clue what sort of clothing to buy. The life she had lived until now had not included any need for formal apparel.

Barely more than an hour and a half later, Alana found herself modelling a floral dress and jacket that she believed would do very well for the civil wedding. She and Ares had contrived in the politest and chilliest of terms to fight quite a bit over her clothes selections. Unopposed, Ares would

have shoved her into fashion far too old and staid
for her tastes. She suspected that Ares socialised
with women around a decade older than she was,
for that classic tailored look was rarely what the
average young woman in her early twenties sought.

Initially seated with Ares in the opulent private
viewing room while svelte models strolled out in
front of them on the little catwalk to show off gar-
ments, Alana had had a couple of glasses of the
complimentary champagne brought to them. She
could feel that faint buzz in her bloodstream and
it made her feel a little more daring than normal
as she strutted out on the catwalk in her bright
dress, doffing the jacket like a professional and
whirling round to let the skirt flip out round her
slender legs. Ares stared at her as though he were
transfixed, those stunning eyes of his amber gold
as a predatory jungle cat's aglow below the lights.

'You have the most amazing eyes,' Alana told
him chattily from the very edge of the catwalk,
which was the closest she could get to him without stepping down to his level and in the very high
heels she wore she didn't trust her balance.

Ares canted up a satirical black brow, cool
as ice, not even a hint of a smile, and Alana just
laughed.

'What?' Ares queried levelly while he thought
that in all his life he had never seen a more gor-

geous woman than Alana in *that* dress. He had insisted that it was too flamboyant and too short when she first showed it to him. Although he had not withheld his strong opinions, she had pretty much ignored his advice, which had disconcerted him. Yet in the flesh, clad in that dress she reminded him of a glorious bouquet of tropical flowers and she did have the most stupendous legs to show off. The golden sheet of her hair had fallen untidily round her flushed face when she twirled, lighting up green eyes like stars and a rosy pillowy mouth that was almost more temptation than he could withstand in that instant.

'I know we're having a register office do with no frills,' Alana continued. 'But this looks kind of bridal in a very *small* way.' As she held up her hand and two fingers measured the very tininess of that bridal element to minimise it for his sensitive benefit, she lurched at the edge of the catwalk and, before she could fall and hurt herself, Ares lunged up out of his seat and caught her in mid-air.

'How the heck did you move that fast?' Alana gasped in amazement. 'I mean, you were in your seat and then you grabbed me—'

'I saved you from tripping,' Ares slotted in a touch raggedly, endeavouring to make his arms lower to put her down on her feet, but that amount of help wasn't happening when his gaze was locked to hers. Not when the desire he saw in her eyes was the exact same as the lusty pulse roaring through his big, powerful body. He knew he shouldn't touch her. He knew he should put her down…but he *didn't*.

'Just do it,' she said simply, and he knew he shouldn't be listening either but when she tilted her head back a little and her velvety soft lips parted in clear invitation, any logic and restraint Ares retained simply tanked. He bent his head, and he kissed her. He took his time about it too. If there was only ever likely to be one single kiss, he fully intended to make a meal of the experience.

Ares had looked at her as though she could walk on water. Alana loved it. No man had ever · looked at her like that, as though she were beautiful, special, and insanely sexy. Her heart was hammering so hard at the strength of the arms holding her against his lean, muscular frame that she could hardly breathe. He was so strong, so fast on his feet, so totally amazing when his stunning dark golden eyes held hers fast. Just at the moment when she was afraid her heart would pound the whole way out of her chest, he brought his mouth down on hers and steadied his hold on her, moving somewhere. Right at that point, she didn't care where he was moving, only that he did what every greedy cell in her body demanded and kissed her.

Ares sat back down in his seat and kissed her.
She tasted so good, it blew his mind. He didn't
usually kiss women. It was too intimate, too romantic, too personal. He did everything else but
he didn't kiss, a little private quirk, he had often
smoothly excused himself when taxed with that
aversion. But when he cradled her cheekbones and
held Alana imprisoned in his arms on his lap, Ares
was for once unruffled by breaking his own code
of rules. There were so many rules in Ares's life.
He did *everything* according to the rules. He kept
himself safe that way. He protected his assets that
way. He ensured that he would never ever be vulnerable to another person again.

He knew how to kiss, he knew how to kiss so
well that at first contact with the hard brush of
his lips across hers Alana's head spun as though
she were on a merry-go-round. It was incredibly,
smoulderingly sexy when his lips gently, firmly
parted hers and his tongue invaded with precision,
sending a shower of fireworks cascading wildly
through her body and lightening up pulse points
she had never felt before. In fact, she had never
felt sexual hunger like it, so it was an enormous
shock when Ares, without the smallest warning,
brought that kiss to an abrupt end. He dragged his
mouth from hers, flipped her upright and stood her
between his spread thighs as if she were a doll.

'We're not doing this,' he breathed hoarsely, a faint dark edge of colour scoring his cheekbones. 'Not you and me together. That *can't* happen…do you understand?'

Shell-shocked by the speed at which that moment of closeness had been severed, Alana nodded numbly. No, she didn't understand, she didn't understand at all, only that Ares looked tense, angry, and unhappy and she didn't like that either. It made her feel guilty, like some fatal temptress who had somehow lured a man into doing what he did not want to do.

'I'm sorry,' she said automatically.

'You didn't do anything. It was *all* me,' Ares asserted, his wide sensual mouth now taut with disapproval. 'I took advantage. You don't let me do that ever again. You say *no*.'

'I say no,' Alana repeated obediently, keen to say anything that would bring the mortifying lecture to an end. 'Got it.'

Ares watched her back away from him as if she were retreating from the lion's den and he expelled a shuddering breath. She was flushed and tossed, her award-winning mouth swollen, her eyes wide and dark with distress and, for the first time in his life since he had become an adult, Ares felt seriously bad for something he had done. Way too young, way too innocent for him, he reminded himself fiercely.

'I messed up your hair,' Alana warned him belatedly. 'You should tidy it.'

'Try on the next outfit. That dress is a definite buy,' Ares told her, prodding her back into role in the hope that while she was changing he would somehow magically work out why he had succumbed so easily to temptation.

'Alana…?' He spoke quietly before she could disappear from view.

She turned back, eyes evading his, no longer lit up like stars, he reminded himself crushingly. 'Yes?'

'Are you a virgin? I know it's a very personal question, and I apologise for asking, but I really would like to know,' Ares murmured in an undertone.

Alana froze and felt her face burn like a bonfire but, now that he had kissed her, she didn't see why she shouldn't answer. 'Yes.'

As she vanished from view to change, Ares breathed in deep on that confirmation, assailed by a variety of very particular reactions. Virginity should be the equivalent of a suit of armour on his terms. It should mean that he would never touch her again, he assured himself resolutely. No honourable male would do anything less when there was no possibility of their relationship going anywhere.

Theos…how had he contrived to *do* this to himself? An own goal of outrageous efficiency? Saddle himself with the one woman he could barely keep his hands off? He should let her go; he knew he should, but he also knew that he couldn't face doing that either. She was safer with him, he told himself, especially now that he *knew*. He would never take advantage of her again. He might be ruthless in business, but he would not be unscrupulous in his private life. It crossed his mind then that, until Alana had thrust herself into his company on that Italian lake front, he hadn't *had* a private life. Occasional, perfunctory, invariably forgettable sex didn't count, and he had no family either.

'It's lovely here. I'll be fine,' Alana declared a couple of hours later as she surveyed the view of the Thames from the balcony, her back turned to him.

Ares had delivered her like a surplus parcel to a beautiful luxury apartment, fully furnished and with a kitchen already stocked with food. She didn't mind being on her own, of course she didn't.

'What about Christmas?' she asked him abruptly, half turning round. 'It's next week and I'm not staying here alone.'

'I don't do the festive season,' Ares parried without any expression at all.

'I'll go home, then, for a couple of days, play the gooseberry for Enzo and Skye,' Alana replied cheerfully, refusing to give way to disappointment. 'I can't miss seeing the children.'

Ares didn't want her leaving London before the wedding. He didn't want to spend any more time with her either, however, lest his once legendary discipline slip again. He forced back his distinct unease at the prospect of her being that far away from him as opposed to being just across the city and jerked his chin in acknowledgement without comment. It was the lesser of two evils, he told himself squarely.

Alana studied him. He revealed nothing. His classic bronzed features could have been carved from ice, his beautiful eyes veiled and narrowed. The kiss had definitely been a mistake. She felt vaguely as though she had a force field around her because he had kept his distance with such pronounced care since then.

'Is there someone else in your life?' she asked baldly, needing to know, refusing to back off to the extent that she didn't dare even ask.

Ares expelled his breath in a slow measured hiss. 'No. But *us*—this is business and you know that.'

'You're the one who broke the contract,' Alana

reminded him with unhidden satisfaction. 'If it's business then let's be sure that we *both* stick to business boundaries.'

Ares could not recall the last time anyone had confronted him with a mistake. Not only did he rarely make a mistake, but also most were sufficiently intimidated by him not to mention it if he did. Why the rock-solid detachment and gravity he wore like a defensive shield didn't work on Alana Davison he could not comprehend.

'Obviously,' he agreed, refusing to rise to that bait that she had tossed out, hoping, he guessed, to involve him in an argument. He wasn't that predictable, at least, he *refused* to be that predictable. 'I'll text you the time and place of the ceremony. If there is anything more you require—relating to the contract—you can contact my lawyers or me but I'm very busy.'

Alana heaved a sigh. 'I'm unlikely to contact you before the wedding. I need nothing and I have nothing to say.'

Ares allowed himself one last lingering look at her. She wore one of the new outfits, a short full skirt teamed with a dusky blue sweater and a leather jacket, complete with knee-high boots. He couldn't even steal a fleeting glance at her without imagining himself pinning her to the nearest surface, be it horizontal or vertical, he wasn't fussy. On the drive to the apartment the amount of erotic imagery that had engulfed his normally disciplined brain had appalled him. It felt horribly as though she were infiltrating him in some way and he detested it. He was walking in the other direction, doing what he knew he had to do to be logical, and only for a split second did he contemplate the reckless option of diving head first into trouble with her. He was too clever for that, he assured himself, too sensible…

Ten days later, Alana contemplated her reflection in the mirror. The dress was very pretty, very flattering. It was her wedding day and she had no nerves. Why would she have? It wasn't a real wedding in the bridal sense. It was a fake, a pretence, nothing more. She had hardened her heart against Ares Sarris. He had closed her out, backed off, spelt out his indifference. *Not even a text?* Well, she would show him that nobody could be any more indifferent than she could be.

The kiss? She had lain awake a few nights recalling how she had felt and then she had shut that down fast. It had been a mistake. For him and for her, a blurring of the firm lines between them. But it tickled Alana pink that *he* had broken their contract first. He wasn't supposed to touch her in any sexual manner and he had smashed his own rule with raw enthusiasm. Put that in your pipe and smoke it, Mr Sarris, she thought childishly, her head swimming a little.

'Are you sure you're feeling well enough for this today?' Skye pressed from her seat on the bed. 'I wish you'd gone to the doctor as I asked you to do—'

'It's just a cold, Skye, not pneumonia.' Alana sighed, her throat aching like her head and she had a bit of a cough. Her muscles were aching a little too. That was all though, certainly not sufficient reason to cancel the wedding that she was being paid to show up at and participate in.

In any case, she wanted the wedding bit done and dusted and then she believed she would feel better, feel more like herself than she had of recent. Her spirits had stayed low even over Christmas with Skye, Enzo, and the kids, when she was normally on top of the world. She didn't know why she was feeling down and continually reminded herself that that ghastly debt was gone now and that soon she would be able to move forward in her life again to a future full of exciting possibilities.

Skye, in full maternal mode, leapt up to rest cool fingers on Alana's brow. 'You're *definitely* running a temperature.'

'I'm OK,' Alana insisted, leaving the bedroom. 'Let's join Enzo. We're getting boring in here.'

'You look great,' her brother-in-law told her carelessly, visibly as certain as a man could be that this was no normal wedding. 'We should leave. Traffic might hold us up.'

Alana suspected that Ares would not be expecting her to have brought guests, but she didn't much care. In any case, her relatives were leaving as soon as the ceremony was complete because Enzo had an important dinner to attend in Italy and he and Skye and the kids were all flying there together. Enzo was so attached to her sister that he took her virtually everywhere with him and Alana admired their closeness as a couple. That was *her* blueprint for the future: finding a guy for herself who would treat her the way Enzo treated Skye. Or even as her stepdad had treated her mother, she thought absently as Enzo's limo nosed through the morning traffic, although she didn't want a man with a gambling problem. She realised that she was finding it difficult to concentrate and her mind was drifting aimlessly.

There was a crush of people in the foyer of the register office. Most of them appeared to belong to Ares's security team and she recognised Edwin Graves, the older man, who was Ares's senior lawyer. She saw the top of Ares's silvery fair head towering over everyone else's and refused to let herself even look in his direction. Let him find out what it was like to be shoved out in the cold and ignored!

Ares scrutinised his bride. Long blonde hair bundled up in some dignified topknot. It didn't suit her. She was just a little bit too thin as well, he decided, noting the almost gaunt aspect of her facial bones. Even so, nothing could dim the loveliness of her face, he conceded, thinking, though, that she had rather overdone it with the rouge. He knew he was being deliberately critical because in some indefinable way he had missed her. Missed that bright novelty freshness that could be so inexplicably appealing. He couldn't explain that oddity to his own satisfaction when he barely knew her and had only recently met her. He tensed in surprise when Enzo Durante appeared in front of him.

'Thought you might appreciate a couple of family witnesses,' Enzo drawled casually. 'But don't worry, we're not staying. We're flying to Italy as soon as this is done.'

Ares's spine tightened. Sixth sense warned him that Enzo knew it wasn't a real wedding. He wasn't even trying to hide the fact. Alana had talked, he was convinced of it but, unusually, he found that he didn't much care. Enzo was no gossip and the bridal family's presence at the wedding did lend validity to the proceedings.

'Look after Alana,' Enzo murmured coolly. 'She's very precious to my wife and her siblings.'

'Alana will come to no harm,' Ares stated with finality, getting really antsy as he looked past Enzo to see his bride *still* not looking at him. Was she trying to make some point? Sulking with him? Offended for some reason? And why did he care either way? Why was he even wondering?

'It's time,' Ares declared, stepping forward to place his hand on Alana's wrist.

'Is it?' She shook her arm free and stalked ahead of him through the doors being held open for their arrival.

In front of the celebrant, he was close enough to Alana to see that what he had assumed was rouge was in fact high colour in her cheeks and it was so obvious because she was deadly pale. He grasped her hand to thread on the wedding ring, a plaited diamond-studded platinum circle that was too large for her, he registered in exasperation, knowing that that was a detail he had overlooked. She hooked her finger round it to keep it on and laughed and then she started coughing and dug out a tissue and he watched her slender shoulders shake as she struggled to stop coughing.

'You're unwell,' Ares said as they walked back out again and she had virtually no memory of the ceremony, merely the drone of a voice in front of her and the stupid ring threatening to fall back off her finger again.

'I'm fine.' Her voice was muffled by the embrace of her sister, who was muttering apologetically that she and Enzo had to leave.

Enzo hugged her as well and Ares thought that was too familiar now that Alana was his wife. A family interaction, he censured himself, the kind of platonic affection he had no experience of being around.

As the other couple departed, Alana slung him a surprised glance. 'You're *still* here?'

Ares froze at that provocative sally.

'Goodbye, Ares,' Alana framed, holding her head high, barely knowing what she was saying because she was feeling so dreadful, weak and sweaty that she wanted to melt into the floor beneath her and vanish.

Before he could even react, she turned away and moved a few steps and then she just dropped into a crumpled heap of bright floral fabric.

'My goodness,' his highly conservative lawyer, Edwin, commented. 'I suppose we'll have to drop her off at some private clinic. At least she made it through the ceremony though.'

Ares stooped and snatched up his unconscious bride from the floor in a hasty movement and locked both arms securely round her. 'I'm not dropping her off anywhere.'

Edwin's brows rose high. 'But—'

'If Alana's ill, she's my responsibility until she's well again,' he announced and, angling his head at his security team, he strode out of the register office onto the pavement, unconcerned by the stares he was attracting for the first time in his life.

CHAPTER FOUR

IT WAS A NIGHTMARE. Even asleep, Alana knew she was having a nightmare. She was trapped in a strange house with endless rooms, and she was running and running and something terrifying was chasing her. Her heart was pounding, her muscles burning as she cried out in fear.

'It's only a dream,' a deep, dark voice murmured soothingly.

Alana felt heavy and unspeakably exhausted and her eyelids were too weighted even to lift. She wondered dimly what was wrong with her but it didn't feel important enough to mention when her brain was a swamp.

A hand grasped her limp fingers where they lay splayed on the cover. 'You will feel better tomorrow,' the voice assured her with impressive confidence. 'It's your temperature. You have a fever. It is probably causing the nightmares.'

And she knew right then that the voice belonged

to Ares. Only Ares would give her that much detail when she was beyond caring and yet the very knowledge that he was with her was a comfort because somehow she *knew* that he would deal with any problem with the utmost efficiency. 'I'm ill,' she mumbled as a more pressing need made itself known to her.

'You have influenza.'

You say flu, she wanted to tell him, but she didn't have the energy and she simply sighed as she shuffled her legs across the bed to find the edge, wondering then why Ares was around when she was in a bed, of all things. She attempted to roll her heavy body.

'What are you trying to do?' Ares demanded, sounding tried beyond measure, making her feel guilty.

'Bathroom,' she said curtly, mortified by that necessity.

Ares gazed down at her with impatience, pushed back the duvet and scooped up her slight body. He had got used to carrying her around and now it cost him not a thought to do it. She weighed far less than she should. The doctor had spelt that out to him in rather accusing terms, as though it were his fault that his wife was so skinny. Maybe she had assumed he was one of those men obsessed with having only a very thin partner. Well, he wasn't, he thought, tucking in one pale slender arm with great care as he strode into the adjoining bathroom and settled her down.

In astonishment at having been lifted in such a way, Alana opened her eyes for the first time and she focused dizzily on a tiled floor and her own bare feet. Her hands slid down over fabric and she studied it in amazement. She was in a nightdress, she who never wore nightdresses, who was a vest and shorts girl, and all she could think about then was how she had got out of her clothes and into a nightdress when she didn't even know where she was.

'Where am I?' she mumbled.

'My home where you are safe.'

She lifted her head enough to focus on bare brown male feet, nicely shaped feet too, she acknowledged abstractedly, noting the hem of jeans visible. Ares in jeans? She really wanted to see that because he was always in a suit and she could imagine him going to bed in a suit like a vampire retiring to his coffin. 'My brain's dead,' she complained of that piece of nonsense.

'Because you're ill.'

Not so ill that she wanted a man in the bathroom with her, she thought fiercely. 'Go! Close the door. Leave me alone.'

'You're not well enough to be left alone,' Ares informed her stubbornly.

With immense effort, Alana threw her head back and finally focused on Ares, barefoot, sheathed in faded jeans and a shirt hanging open on a bronzed torso worthy of a centrefold and a thousand camera flashes. It was to her credit that she didn't get sidetracked by the view and still hissed, 'Says who? Get out of here!'

As soon as the door closed on his exit, Alana slumped and slowly took care of herself, crawling across a cold floor to lever herself up by a cupboard to a sink. As she clumsily washed her hands, splashed water on her hot face and buried her face in a towel, she remembered that they had got married. She looked at her hand but her finger was bare. Oh, heavens, had she already lost that ring that had looked as though it had cost a king's ransom?

As she began to open the door, it opened for her and Ares scooped her up again as if it were the easiest thing in the world to lift a fully grown adult woman. He settled her back into the bed, fixed the pillows, tugged the duvet over her while her green eyes clung to his hard bronzed features in a daze. 'I've lost the wedding ring.'

'It was falling off. I removed it and I'm having it resized,' Ares explained, lifting a glass of water with a straw to angle it at her helpfully for her to drink before retreating to an armchair within a few feet of the bed.

'What time is it?'

'It's the middle of the night. Go back to sleep.'

Her troubled gaze rested on him. It might be the middle of the night, but Ares Sarris radiated energy just the same as usual and betrayed not a hint of emotion. 'I'm being a nuisance,' she began uneasily.

'You're my wife. You're my nuisance for the moment,' Ares retorted crisply.

'You've got no tact,' Alana framed drowsily.

'And you're *surprised*?'

'You still look like an angel,' she whispered, almost mesmerised by the light from the lamp that gilded his hair and threw his perfect features into an intriguing mix of exotic peaks and shadowed hollows.

Even if Alana was plainly still feverish, Ares was relieved that she was opening her eyes and talking again. Unconscious, Alana had panicked him just a little. Until the doctor had reassured him, Ares had been deeply concerned...*obviously*. Married one day and a widower the next might not have fulfilled the will and it would be outrageous to go to such lengths as matrimony only to be thwarted by a dying bride. On another level,

impervious to the ruthlessness of that last thought,
Ares watched her sleep, scanning the silky golden
hair tangled across the pillow, the curling lashes
separating her determined little nose above the
peachy softness of that mouth he had tasted with
such forbidden pleasure. He almost smiled as he
opened his laptop, deeming it safe to work now
that she had made what he viewed as her very first
step in the recovery process.

A nurse in a uniform greeted Alana when she
wakened later the following day.

'I'm your nurse, Fay,' she said cheerfully with
a smile.

'Where's…er…?' Alana framed, lying still as
she realised she felt too weak to push up against
the pillows.

'Your husband? Probably sleeping, Mrs Sarris. From what the staff told me, he was so worried about you that he sat up all night with you.'

Alana's lips rounded into a soft 'oh' of surprise,
but her heart warmed. Ares had worried about
her. Presumably, that was why he had been in her
room when she'd surfaced in the middle of the
night. Even though it was only a dose of the flu,
she could understand why he had been concerned
when she had fainted the way she had, wincing at
what a show she must have made of them collaps-
ing like that in a public place.

Fay asked her if she would like some breakfast.

'I'm not hungry—'

'Dr Melrose is concerned that you have missed so many meals and that you still have little appetite,' Fay said. 'It would be great if you could try to eat something. Toast?'

Alana nodded absently.

Living in at the hotel, she had got thinner, she conceded, probably because she worked long hours and, when she wasn't working in what was often a very physical job, she ate whatever was cheapest and quickest to prepare in the small kitchen in the staff quarters.

'Who's Dr Melrose?' she asked.

'She's very nice. Your husband brought her in to check you over yesterday. I arrived about the same time and I put you to bed.'

Alana sank back into her huge bed and dully surveyed a bedroom the size of a football pitch. If this was Ares's home, he lived in incredibly opulent style. At least he hadn't dared to undress her and put her into the gothic nightdress. Last night she had been so pale and washed out in appearance she had resembled a corpse in her white shroud. Luckily, she was still feeling too unwell to care what she looked like.

Fay switched on the giant television on the wall and brought her the controls. 'This is the most fabulous house I have ever been in,' she confided in some excitement, but Alana was already sliding back into sleep again, exhausted by her time awake.

Over the following couple of days, there were times that Alana didn't know whether she was asleep or in a waking dream but slowly, far more slowly than she would have liked, she began feeling better. There were glimpses of Ares in her recent memories and she didn't know whether they were real or imagined. She had an image of him gazing down at her from his great height, dark golden eyes troubled as she tossed and turned. She had another image of him working at a laptop while he sat by the window and looking up, finding her staring, he had said, 'You should eat something.'

'Not hungry,' she had told him hoarsely as he'd brought the straw in the water glass within reach of her parched lips.

'Some women would eat just to please me,' he had told her with assurance.

Her nose had wrinkled. 'Not that desperate,' she had mumbled and he had laughed.

Had that exchange really happened? she wondered now that she felt stronger and her appetite had returned. Breakfast arrived very soon after Fay had ordered it by phone. It came on a trolley as though she were in a hotel and two servers accompanied it, one carting a lap tray, which was unfurled for her use and soon furnished with flowers and cutlery, the other showing off the choices on the trolley. A lot more than tea and toast had been prepared. There was oatmeal, eggs, toast, pastries, fruit and, like Fay, everyone was so patently keen for her to eat that she duly took the eggs even though she couldn't eat very much. Soon after that, the female doctor called in, a serious young woman, who talked to her about good nutrition.

Having slept the afternoon away, Alana felt well enough to try out the rainwater shower in the bathroom with Fay nearby in case she became dizzy. Refreshed, she was disconcerted when the nurse informed her that the dressing room off the bedroom was packed with her clothes, which had arrived two days earlier. Alana discovered that her new wardrobe and her own small stock of clothes were now combined. Ares must've had the apartment she had been using cleared and her possessions transferred to his home. Clad in shorts and a vest, her hair dried at Fay's insistence, she felt better.

Skye phoned her from Italy. 'Good to know that you're making Ares Sarris work at this marriage,' her sister said teasingly.

'What on earth are you talking about?'

'You bridegroom was on the phone to me the day before yesterday for almost half an hour—'

'What did he phone you for?' Alana exclaimed with a frown.

'He's contacted us every day since you fell ill. He's been asking questions and not about business. He had to know what sort of books you read, what sort of movies you like, what you like to eat, what your favourite colours are… Oh, there's no end of detail to what Ares feels that he *needs* to know!' Her sister punctuated that comment with an appreciative giggle. 'So, I haven't worried too much about you being ill, not with your personal doctor and nurse on call, and Ares ready to go to superhuman lengths to ensure that you're well looked after.'

'I'm amazed,' Alana responded honestly.

'I was as well. I thought he was a total iceberg… but underneath there's definitely a thoughtful guy trying to break out. Enzo thinks it's very funny. He used to think Ares was a total stuffed shirt and a grinch and now he's wondering.'

A knock sounded on the door and Fay answered it. Two staff members carried in a table and placed it beside the window. A third brought a dining chair.

'I believe your husband's planning to join you

for dinner,' her nurse told her in an *Aren't-you-a lucky-girl?* tone.

Alana forced a smile. Fake new bride, she reminded herself anxiously. Ironic though, she thought wryly, that Ares had still contrived to spend their official wedding night with her. Presumably his visits were for the benefit of his staff and he was doubtless resenting the hell out of that necessity. After all, the plan had been for a separation immediately after the wedding ceremony. She was already falling down on her *fake* wifely duties, she reflected ruefully. It would be natural for Ares to feel annoyed when she had fallen ill and he had not felt it possible to walk away.

But what was the actual purpose of the bogus wife charade? she finally stopped to wonder with intense curiosity. What could make a male as strong as Ares Sarris resort to such a tactic? That fascinated her.

Alana went into the bathroom to brush her hair, pinch her pale cheeks and use her lip gloss and every step of the way she told herself off for doing so. So, she was attracted to him. No big deal. Adolescent crushes had taught her that a girl didn't always get what she wanted, especially if he was a teen idol in a band. That was life and Ares Sarris had more choice of female company than most, not to mention the fact that he preferred to abide by their contract and was determined not to break it. Even though he already *had* in a small way with that kiss? Alana went pink, recalling that surge of wicked uncensored hunger that had flooded her and squirming at the recollection. She was less impressed remembering Ares's cool retreat in the aftermath.

Ares strode through the door and her nurse studied him with glazed appreciation written all over her face. Yes, he was very, very good-looking, especially with a five o'clock shadow of stubble enhancing his strong jawline. Even Alana was riveted to her pillows, just taking in the whole vibrant vision of her warrior angel. Silvery hair ruffled over that classic hard-boned face, dark deep-set eyes with a hint of gold, a dark formal business suit perfectly tailored to his lean muscular frame. She watched him dismiss her nurse, barely breaking his stride, and then the food arrived along with what appeared to be deliveries, which were settled onto the foot of her bed.

'What's all this?' she asked in the midst of the chaos of food being served and Ares sinking fluidly down into his chair emanating that calm, controlled assurance that was uniquely his.

'I bought you some stuff,' he imparted with an eloquent shift of one lean brown hand. 'You won't be up and about for a few days yet, so I asked your sister what you enjoyed.'

'And what did you get me?'

Ares arose again to tip out a bag of books, bright cover designs catching her eyes, and she almost shrieked in dismay, her fingers clenching round one at the sight of a half-naked male with wings and a sword. Heat burned up from the centre of her and flushed her entire skin surface.

'Angel romance,' Ares said unnecessarily, trying not to smile, trying not to linger on the recollection of what she had said to him while still feverish. 'A niche concept but, according to your sister, your favourite—'

'I like fantasy books,' Alana acknowledged flatly, averting her gaze from the colourful risqué covers as she crammed them all back into the bag with clumsy hands. If a woman could die from embarrassment, she would have died there and then right in front of him.

'There's a tablet there as well and it's loaded with digital copies. I forgot to ask your sister your reading preference.'

'This is so kind of you. Thank you,' Alana voiced her gratitude between gritted teeth.

Ares lifted another bag. 'And you like to knit…'

Knit? Alana hadn't knitted anything since her school art exam had demanded she produce a handcrafted item. She looked into the bag at beautiful shades of wool and needles and several patterns and her tummy flipped. My goodness, he must think she was a really exciting young woman with her angel romance and her stupid knitting! Couldn't Skye have lied and invented more exciting, glamorous pastimes for her benefit?

'There's other things there.' Ares indicated the bags and sat down at the table where the first course of his meal awaited him. 'I thought if you were feeling up to the challenge, I would take you out of this room for a while.'

'I would love that.' Alana smiled warmly, lifting her knife and fork.

'We'll have our coffee downstairs,' Ares decreed as he leant back in his chair. 'Have you a robe?'

Alana pushed away the lap tray and slid out of bed to head for the dressing room.

'There's a new one here,' Ares divulged, rising to indicate the big shallow box still lying at the foot of the bed.

Alana returned to the bed and bent down to open the box. 'Why would you buy me something like that?' she asked uncomfortably.

'I didn't know what you owned in that line.'

Alana went pink, recalling that she had modelled neither the nightwear nor the lingerie for him,

merely choosing sufficient to meet her needs behind closed doors. She shook out a slippery silky
robe in a soft shade of green.

Ares was welded to her every move, his attention roaming from the full firm mounds of her
breasts swelling above the vest neckline to the
pert curve of her bottom before scanning the surprising length of her slender legs. The swelling at
his groin was immediate and intense and his expressive mouth tightened. It annoyed him that he
could still be so susceptible, and it struck him as
a downright unforgivable response while she was
still recovering from illness.

Alana tied the sash on the robe and walked to
the door.

'Slippers?'

'I don't have any. Didn't think of them.'

Ares opened the door and then bent down to
lift her up into his arms.

'What on earth are you doing?'

'It's a lengthy walk and you're not that fit yet,'
Ares told her levelly.

'I'm fine.'

'Your sister admitted that even if you were on
the brink of death you would still insist that you
are *fine*. I'm not listening,' Ares declared, walking down a wide staircase with her firmly clasped
in his arms.

'You're too bossy and pushy for me,' Alana protested, striving to hold her own and act as casually as he did and as though the intimacy of his hold were not a trial to her.

But then possibly he was less sensitive and self-conscious than she was. But she could *feel* the heat of his broad chest all along one side of her body, smell the faint tang of his cologne and was almost within touching distance of his outrageously perfect mouth. As he strode through an echoing hall, she breathed in deep, ashamed of the prickling sting of her nipples and the surge of heat between her thighs.

'This is the orangery,' Ares informed her as he laid her down on an upholstered chaise longue in a large room walled with lush indoor plants and a line of windows overlooking a lit winter terrace. 'My housekeeper is bringing coffee for me and hot chocolate for you.'

'Skye must've talked her head off to you.' Alana sighed, colouring. 'But I'm almost on my feet again, so you must be relieved about that—'

'You can't leave until your health is fully restored,' Ares slotted in quietly.

'I feel like *your* responsibility now,' Alana gathered. 'And you take your responsibilities very seriously.'

'That is a trait I am proud to possess.'

'But I'm not your responsibility...well, at least only on paper,' Alana reasoned, stiffening when Ares raised a dark brow of silent disagreement. 'It's not as though we are a genuine husband and wife,' she added in a whisper, mindful of the risk of being overheard.

An older woman appeared with a tray.

Alana cradled her ornamental china cup of chocolate in one hand while nibbling at a tiny truffle cake. 'Skye told you about my love of truffles as well,' she groaned. 'And you're spoiling me.' As if she were a sick child, she thought in powerful chagrin.

'You deserve to be spoiled after the experience you have had.'

'No, I don't!' Alana argued with sudden vehemence, green eyes wide. 'I let you down. I caught the flu and forced you to change all your plans.'

Ares watched her stretch out on the sofa, little pink toes extended. She had tiny feet, tiny hands, dainty narrow wrists and ankles. The sash on the robe had loosened, parting the edges of the robe, treating him to a view of pointed nipples indenting her flimsy top. Ares tensed and addressed his attention to the sickly-sweet treats that had vanished from the plate at speed and again he tried hard not to smile, he who so rarely smiled. She amused him, that was all. There was something so essentially feminine about her. He couldn't quite work out what it was or why she exuded incredible sex appeal without making the smallest effort. He only knew that he resolutely refused to succumb to that appeal.

'Ares?' Alana said. 'You didn't answer me—'

'It's not your fault that you fell ill,' Ares slotted in drily. 'But we won't be revisiting my original terms in the contract until I believe that you have fully regained your health.'

'Is that so?' Even to her own ears, her tone sounded tart but he made her speak like that, she conceded wryly. He was such a know-it-all, really couldn't help being like that because she reckoned he was accustomed to being the cleverest person in most rooms. And she could live with that, kind of understood it. What she couldn't live with was the way he tried to act as though the attraction between them didn't exist.

That drove her insane. For her, it wasn't simply physical attraction and she knew that. Alana had never hidden from her own feelings. Ares Sarris mesmerised her as thoroughly as a snake charmer did a snake. When he was around, she couldn't take her eyes off him and her heart pounded as though she were running. And the whole time in the background of her brain she was experiencing this wild edge-of-the-seat excitement she couldn't quell just because he was with her. She supposed it was an infatuation, but she wasn't a kid any longer and she suspected she was falling in love for the very first time and that scared and thrilled her in equal proportions.

A slanting grin slashed Ares's lean bronzed features without warning, chasing the air of studious gravity he usually wore. 'I think we both know how much I enjoy being what you call…er…bossy. But I do have a surprise for you—'

'Everything you do is a surprise!' Alana told him truthfully, still reeling from that sudden almost boyish grin and a level of charisma that blew every rational thought right out of her head.

'I believe you're strong enough to travel now. We're flying to my property in Abu Dhabi tomorrow, where you will enjoy some winter sun and complete your recovery process,' Ares informed her smoothly. 'After that, we will return to fulfilling our contract as it was written.'

CHAPTER FIVE

ONLY TWENTY-FOUR HOURS LATER, Alana chattered to her sister on her mobile phone while resting back on a lounger on a sun-drenched terrace lapped by the turquoise waters of the Persian Gulf. It was idyllic. From indoors, Ares was absently listening to that tone of bubbling energy and pleasure that he most enjoyed hearing in her voice. Delighting Alana gave him a kick and he didn't know why.

'It's the most amazing house. It's right on a private beach and it's built of wood and stone,' Alana was carolling. 'And it has this bathroom with a circular bath that overlooks the beach. I can't wait to get into it! Ares has such amazing, good taste. He designed it. Can you believe that? He designed it himself!'

Ares stopped listening and smiled as he worked. She was happy. When she had been ill, she had been miserable, that soft mouth down-curved, those bright eyes dull and lifeless. He had felt guilty about that. He had wanted to see her smile again and she hadn't stopped smiling since his private jet had landed in the UAE. She had been leaning out of windows, pointing at stuff, talking him to death by asking constant questions, basically showing off how youthful she still was with her enthusiasm for everything, he conceded ruefully. It was cute, *she* was cute, but basically only the way a puppy or kitten was cute, nothing more personal than that, he assured himself confidently.

'Sometimes you're very quiet,' Alana complained over dinner after her fifth conversational sally had crashed and burned. She wanted to slap him because her temper was on a hair trigger. All day, Ares had tuned her out as though she were a television playing in the background. It drove her mad. How could he *do* that? How could he ignore the chemical attraction that lit her up inside like a light installation when they were together? How could he behave as though it weren't happening? And yet when he looked at her directly, every time she *knew* that he wasn't indifferent to her. It was just there in his eyes, the curve of his lips, the tilt of his head. He couldn't hide *everything* from her.

Alana didn't understand what that stupid contract had to do with anything in the *real* world. That contract was primarily to protect Ares's wealth, that was what she had read in all those weighty paragraphs of legalese that she had ultimately only given a cursory read because it would genuinely have taken her hours to properly go through such a long document. At the heart of that contract, however, they were still two adult, single human beings, both of them surely free to do as they liked. Only Ares flatly refused in any field of his life to do as he liked if he believed that doing so would be unwise. Sadly, when it came to her, Ares had a will as strong as forged iron.

Ares contrived to smile across the table at the air of exasperation stamped on her lovely expressive face. 'When I have a business problem, I tend to be very quiet while I consider it.'

Having finished eating, Alana sprang upright. 'Well, you should have explained that sooner!'

'It's antisocial to be like that but I've *always* been like that,' Ares admitted levelly, neither apologising nor soothing her ruffled feathers, because he was who he was.

'Well, I've used up *my* day's allowance of sociability,' Alana countered squarely. 'You had your chance to be company and you blew it… I'm going for a bath!'

'I'll see you tomorrow, then.' Ares's dark golden eyes glittered with ferocious appreciation as he watched her stalk sassily out of the dining room. He liked her cheek. In the past ten and more years, nobody but her had ever dared to be cheeky with him. Possibly it would've surprised her to learn that he found her incredibly entertaining and stimulating company. After all, it had surprised *him*. She sizzled and boiled with emotions like a miniature volcano and displayed it all on her beautiful face. She was his polar opposite in personality.

In the bedroom next door to Alana's, he peeled off his suit, resolving to put on shorts and a T-shirt the next day before Alana criticised him again for failing to relax his dress code. He froze. Why was he taking account of *her* preferences? Ares had always moved to his own beat, stubbornly opposed to meeting other people's wishes and standards. He fell still and then dropped his shirt with a chuckle. Obviously, he was *humouring* her, the same way people indulged children and pets, he told himself.

The shriek that broke the silence cut through the wall between their bedrooms and acted like an enemy air-raid siren on Ares. In his boxers, he raced out of the room and into hers and straight into the bathroom…where she was bouncing around stark naked and sobbing and clutching at her foot.

'My toe!' she gasped tragically.

Ares averted his gaze from her nudity, but not quite before he had appreciated that the richer protein-based diet in his London home had made her a touch less slender. He snatched up a giant towel and wrapped her in it while she continued to try and hop around like a frantic one-legged bunny rabbit being chased by a shotgun. In frustration, Ares lifted her protesting body out of the bathroom and sank down on the edge of the bed with her on his lap. He smoothed her foot with a firm hold and soothing stroking fingers over her stubby little toes.

He touched her with a gentle kindness nobody who looked at him would be aware he was even capable of demonstrating, Alana conceded. He had been so good to her while she was ill and when they had arrived at the fabulous villa, it had felt ridiculously like a honeymoon destination and as if they were normal newly marrieds.

She blinked back the tears that had engulfed her and started to apologise for the fuss she had made. And then, she thought, *No, I'm not doing this, I'm not doing fake when I've finally got his arms round me again.*

Her hand stretched up to slowly push her fingers into his tousled silvery fair hair and hold him fast. Her other hand found its own path up to the sensual fullness of his lower lip and scored along it.

'What are you doing?' Ares asked icily.

But Alana knew that icy detachment he called up at will was only superficial, certainly not anything that she believed she needed to worry about. His stunning eyes locked to hers. 'Alana—'

'You're faking disinterest,' Alana muttered. 'Stop it! Stop acting like I'm assaulting you! You want me just as much as I want you. I'm not so stupid that I can't see that. I don't know why you're doing it. I don't understand why you're pushing me away yet keeping me so close…'

And within a split second, Ares caved in to the sheer temptation of her because he didn't understand either and he really, *really* didn't want to talk about it and if he kissed her, at least, she wouldn't be asking him for answers he couldn't give her. His mouth claimed her parted lips while she was still talking and every atom of the raw hunger he had suppressed flooded through that first kiss like a dangerous storm warning.

Alana surfaced dizzily to find herself prone on the bed. She went back into the kiss after a necessary intake of oxygen and every skin cell was screaming with joy that Ares had finally dropped his walls and surrendered to their mutual chemistry. She knew that she was encouraging him but she also knew that he had started it all with that first kiss. Until then, she had held back, she had suppressed her response to him but that first kiss had set that attraction free and Alana had never been too timid or afraid to go after what she wanted.

It was one of those very rare occasions when Ares wasn't thinking, indeed he was refusing to think. He *knew* that if he started thinking he would stop and come up with all the very good reasons why he should *not* become intimate with Alana Davison. He arranged her on the bed with precision and great care and he looked at her, lying there, letting him look with that intoxicating smile of hers and not a hint of shyness. He enjoyed that view so very much that for the first time ever he understood why lovers took naked photos of each other, an act that had previously struck him as the worst and lowest of aberrations.

'Why are you staring at me? Is there something wrong?' Alana gasped, emerald eyes suddenly anxious.

'You're a fantasy,' Ares framed, not entirely convinced that that *was* him speaking, but she was smiling again, so it really did not matter if he had turned into some Jekyll and Hyde twin-natured creature who didn't know what he was doing or saying. He liked it when she smiled. It was that simple.

And then Ares claimed her lips again and Alana was in heaven because Ares was incredibly good at the art of kissing. Certainly, no other male had ever got her so stirred up with kisses and she had never let any other male go travelling with his kisses across the rest of her body. But when it was Ares, everything was different. Every inch of her craved Ares's touch and when he paused to suck at a straining nipple, her hips left the bed and she made a squeaky sound that made him glance up at her in surprise.

'I liked it,' she told him hurriedly, lest he desist in the belief that she hadn't. 'Just lost my voice.'

A wicked grin illuminated his dark features. 'You're very vocal… I like that, *asteri mou*.'

And Alana was discovering that she seemed to like absolutely everything that Ares did to her. Her body no longer felt under her control. Her heart was racing and jumping, her muscles jerking taut. A lean hand stroked her thigh and she was convinced she was about to spontaneously combust. There was a buzz inside her like a battery revving up, but it was a buzz that had been building for days every time Ares looked at her, touched her, spoke to her—her sense of connection to him was that intense. That Ares was finally acknowledging the same reactions felt miraculous and wonderful.

He traced her fine bones and the glorious curves of her with a sense of discovery that was new to him. The creamy smooth skin, the bright green eyes, the soft silky strands of hair. It was just sex, his brain chimed in without warning, and there was never anything remotely special about sex. He *knew* that. He had seen that from his earliest years and the darkness of those times had ensured that he was more careful than most not to attach any deeper emotion to a physical act. That thought cooled his heated blood and he fell back from her, suddenly questioning what he was doing, why he was smashing down barriers that he had always respected, why he wasn't weighing up the potential costs of such unusual behaviour.

'What's up?' Alana lifted her head off the pillow, chilled by that revealing withdrawal, the black lashes lowering to veil his dark eyes to a narrow golden shimmer. 'No, not now,' she muttered, her finger splaying across a satin-smooth bronzed shoulder. 'Don't you dare go inside that head of yours and start brooding and questioning and doubting. I won't have it.'

A reluctant laugh was wrenched from Ares. 'You won't?' he scoffed.

'No because this is *my* big sex scene, not yours,' Alana countered, teasing him in a way she had never imagined she would tease a male, but there was something about Ares's reserve that made her bold. 'Your only responsibility is to make it amazing—'

'Could be a challenge for a man with a virgin,' Ares parried, his dark deep drawl shaking slightly because in a handful of words she had somehow banished the darkness inside him with her own weird gift of light and made him swallow back laughter.

'Am I the first one you've been with?' Alana asked jealously.

'Yes.'

'Then you don't know what you're talking about, so keep quiet,' Alana urged, small hand travelling down over his indented muscular torso in an appreciative caress. 'Lie back. I want a live anatomy lesson—'

Ares grinned and caught her tiny hand in his and gently eased her back again. 'You're not running this show. I am, *asteri mou*,' he assured her, and that shadowy instant of almost stepping back from the brink was conquered by her appeal and forgotten. 'Tonight is for you, *only* for you.'

'I'm not going to be a selfish lover,' Alana objected.

Still smiling, Ares gathered her into his arms and kissed her breathless, revelling in the taste of her, the silky soft delicacy of her skin against his. Alana quivered as he rubbed gently over her prominent nipples, nurturing the sensitivity there to send a dart of heat down between her legs. She squirmed as long skilled fingers traced the damp core of her, gently teased the entrance, delivering a cascade of unfamiliar new sensations that parted her lips on a moan.

His tongue dallied with hers and she writhed as the intensity of sensation gathered like a hot liquid pool low in her belly. He rested her down and kissed and licked a trail down over her quivering length, sliding her thighs further apart. He used his lips on the sensitive bundle of nerves that controlled her and from that point on, everything he did to her was off-the-charts *hot* and so exciting she gasped and writhed and simply lived in the moment. The tension at her core built and built until her climax flamed up through her, leaving her limp in the aftermath.

'That was amazing,' she told him chattily.

'That's my line,' he censured.

'So far, the fun has all been mine,' Alana pointed out.

Ares laughed, dark golden eyes smouldering. 'I don't have fun. I'm a very serious guy.'

She wanted to tell him that he wasn't going to get away with being serious twenty-four-seven with her around, but she wasn't yet sure that he would give her the chance to *be* with him. It was like being on trial, she acknowledged nervously, waiting to see how he reacted to her, what he would want…perhaps, he wouldn't want a repeat or anything else. After all, theirs was not a real marriage, she reminded herself, and it was on paper a marriage without a future.

But from that first kiss, Alana had been entrapped and she had turned off her critical thinking. Instead, she was taking a risk and Ares Sarris was very much an unknown quantity. He was so generous with everything but information. He didn't tell her anything about himself, his life, his background, his feelings. All of it was a closed book and she hated that because she was frantic to know him better and learn exactly what drove him aside from an evident need to make mountains of money.

'We've only begun, *asteri mou*,' Ares husked, leaning over her, dark stubble accentuating his beautifully sculpted pink lips. His narrowed gaze, thickly lined with black lashes, was stunning that close, eyes burnished by every shade of gold just like that night by the lake.

Her heart skipped a beat and she lifted her head and found his mouth again for herself. He released her reddened lips and trailed his own down over her cheeks to her throat and she shivered with reaction, nerve endings awakening where she had not realised they existed.

'I'm not expecting rainbows and kittens,' Alana told him with innate practicality.

'Is that supposed to encourage me to sink to the

level of your low expectations?' Ares enquired lazily as he lowered his lean hips, sliding between her thighs, and she felt him hard and ready at the heart of her. 'That's one challenge I won't be accepting.'

The tender tissue at the heart of her was so wet, he slid against her and a ripple of arousal ran through her afresh. He tugged back her knees and settled her into a more favourable position, rocking over her, grinding down with his hips, stimulating her clitoris with every movement until the hunger began to heat and course through her veins again. He entered her slow and steady and she tipped back more as he spread her knees wider. As he pushed deeper, there was a slight burn that was bearable and then he glided out and into her again, pushing forward, punching through the barrier she had not even guessed still existed. The sharp pain made her rise up and cry out, gritting her teeth hastily on any further noise, chagrin filling her as Ares stilled.

'I hurt you… I'm sorry.' He murmured something in Greek and brushed his lips across her brow in a surprisingly tender gesture .

Well, not so much a fantasy woman any more,' Alana reflected ruefully as he stilled. 'Don't stop,' she urged unevenly. 'It's not hurting now.'

And in a smooth shift of his lean hips he withdrew and then drove into her again and a jolting thrill gripped her, the pleasure receptors at her core reacting to that raw invasion. Her hands rubbed across his strong shoulders and stroked down his smooth, muscular back to grip him. Now she was finding out what sex was all about, not those first moments after all but much more was to be discovered in what followed. His every powerful thrust made her clench her inner muscles round him and the friction sent her excitement racing up the scale. Heart thundering in her ears, she gave herself up to the intoxication, rising up against him, frantic for his driving pace to continue and when she reached the ultimate peak and convulsed again in what felt like a million glittery pieces of drowning pleasure, she was shaken but satisfied as he too shuddered with completion.

Happy, she wrapped round Ares like an octopus.

'I love being close to you like this,' she whispered.

It had been years since anyone had dared to touch Ares without permission, even in bed. He didn't cuddle, he didn't snuggle. Alana's easy affection cut through the drugging glaze of his physical satisfaction. It reminded him that she had none of his emotional damage, that she was *whole* and that he had nothing whatsoever to offer such a woman. She would want love and affection and a family and, not only was he not equipped to meet such needs, but he also knew that he would never seek out such binding ties. In that acceptance of his fatal flaws, Ares dropped instantly from what felt dimly like the heights of some unnamed emotion to rock-bottom reality and, a split second later, he pulled free of Alana and sprang out of the bed.

From the doorway, he looked back at her and momentarily stilled, his powerful bronzed body taut. 'This was wrong for *both* of us,' he told her grimly. 'I'll leave early in the morning and you'll stay for the rest of the week as planned. Next week you'll move into Templegreen, my country house in Surrey.'

'I don't understand *why* it's wrong,' she declared defiantly.

'I won't answer that,' Ares countered tautly.

Alana didn't say anything more. In that moment there didn't seem anything to say that wouldn't invite an even greater humiliation. As the door thudded closed, she was pale as death and chilled to the marrow. She huddled into the cocoon of the sheet and shivered, no longer feeling brave, bright and happy. He had rejected her, indisputably rejected her. There would be no coming back from that. He didn't want what she had to offer and really, when all was said and done, what did she have to offer a male as sophisticated and spoilt for choice as Ares Sarris? It wasn't as though the fact that they were married counted in the balance because Ares had never intended it to be a real marriage. And obviously in the seductress stakes she had struck out badly as well.

She wanted to call her sister and spill her guts in the hope that that outlet would take away some of the anguish building inside her. But some stuff, she acknowledged heavily, wasn't for sharing. She couldn't empty her heart to her sister when Enzo and Skye knew Ares and Enzo did business with him. That wouldn't be fair to Ares when she had been a fully participating partner in everything that had happened between them. Never mind that stupid contract that had already been broken by their intimacy, but she *had* promised not to talk about him, *had* agreed to protect his privacy. And privacy meant more to Ares than to most men. He didn't deserve a punishment for the mistake of having had sex with her, did he?

He was entitled to have sex with a consenting partner and then walk away afterwards if he chose to do so. It was a free world…for Ares, if not for her. That meant that she wasn't entitled to chain him up in a dungeon somewhere and torture him until he agreed to be hers and *only* hers. They were only husband and wife on paper and she didn't have any of the rights of a wife.

What Ares did next was none of her business. He could be with other women if he chose to be with other women. He didn't have to be faithful to her, although *she* had to be faithful to him. Yes, she had read those parts of that iniquitous contract and appreciated that, while he remained essentially free, she remained bound to consider appearances and the onus was on her to conduct herself as the wife of Ares Sarris should at all times. And that meant she was not to do anything that might attract publicity or be seen out in public in the company of other men. Not that anyone but her immediate family and his lawyers even knew that they were married as yet, but she presumed that over time their marriage would become more widely known.

On the score of her behaviour, however, Ares had already contrived to turn her right off the prospect of any sort of involvement with a man. Just then, Alana felt horribly responsible for her own downfall. *She* had wanted Ares from the very first moment she saw him. Admittedly, that had not been why she'd offered to be his fake wife. She had done that because she was in debt and saw no reasonable way of clearing that debt unless she chose to hurt her sister by telling her the unlovely truth about the stepfather she had adored. Whichever way she looked at the current situation, it made her feel guilty. After all, she had married Ares, secretly armed with foolish hopes and dreams that she had next to no chance of fulfilling.

Before they had had actual sex, he had attempted to back off and she had argued him out of that decision, insanely convinced that intimacy would bring down his barriers and give her a chance with him. But all she seemed to have achieved was that Ares had built his walls even higher and was now asserting that anything between them was a mistake. It might not have been a mistake for her but clearly it was for Ares. And that was life, she told herself with helpless self-loathing. You didn't always get what you wanted and people didn't always react as you wished. She had made her best effort and lost. He didn't want her. He was walking away untouched while she felt torn apart and desperately hurt.

And what were these feelings that he had thrown back in her face? No, she wasn't travelling any further down the road of regret. She had had a one-night stand and she had always wanted more for herself, had always hoped that when she finally had sex, it would be within a meaningful relationship. The last laugh was on her for being as naïve as to believe that she could share anything meaningful with Ares Sarris.

* * *

At least she hadn't run the risk of getting pregnant, she consoled herself, thinking of the contraceptive pill she had begun taking a couple of years earlier for her painful periods. Just at that point, she froze in dismay and jumped out of bed in haste to retrieve her handbag and check on her pills. When had she last taken one? It was an effort to concentrate and the answer was not reassuring. It had been *before* the wedding and she had taken none while she was ill, forgetting about them entirely. Even worse, she had changed handbags and come away without the packet.

Apprehension filled her. She assumed that Ares had taken precautions of his own and then she frowned because she couldn't recall any evidence in that field. If they had both been careless, and she was challenged to believe that *he* would have run that risk, where did that leave her? In a stupid panic of ever-increasing worries, she scolded herself. It was foolish to fret about what she couldn't change.

But the damage had already been done. Blinking back stinging tears, Alana lay sleepless most of the night. She finally drifted off out of sheer exhaustion but only after she heard a helicopter arrive and then depart again. She knew then that she was now alone in the villa, aside from the staff.

CHAPTER SIX

ARES FLIPPED VERY slowly through the photos sent by Alana's protection team, magnifying most of them and scrutinising all of them with careful attention to detail. His wife had been enjoying the hell out of herself since his departure. He had never seen any woman smile so much. If he had assumed she would simply rest back on her sunlounger and work on her tan while taking the occasional break to shop until she dropped, he had been very much mistaken. And if he had worried that his sudden exit could have upset or hurt her, he had been equally misguided.

There she was on Saadiyat Island, soaking up the culture at the Louvre Abu Dhabi, stocking up on art supplies from the Manarat al Saadiyat and strolling along a shaded pathway in the garden city of Al Ain. She was perfectly dressed in respect of local mores, chino trousers hugging her long legs, a simple cotton top screening her delectable curves

Dear Reader,

Your opinions are important to us. So if you'll participate in our fast and free "One Minute" Survey, YOU can pick up to four wonderful books that WE pay for when you try the Harlequin Reader Service!

As a leading publisher of women's fiction, we'd love to hear from you. That's why we promise to reward you for completing our survey.

IMPORTANT: Please complete the survey and return it. We'll send your Free Books and a Free Mystery Gift right away. And we pay for shipping and handling too! *We pay for ← EVERYTHING!*

Try **Harlequin® Desire** and get 2 books featuring the worlds of the American elite with juicy plot twists, delicious sensuality and intriguing scandal.

Try **Harlequin Presents® Larger-Print** and get 2 books featuring the glamourous lives of royals and billionaires in a world of exotic locations, where passion knows no bounds.

Or TRY BOTH!

Thank you again for participating in our "One Minute" Survey. It really takes just a minute (or less) to complete the survey... and your free books and gift will be well worth it!

If you continue with your subscription, you can look forward to curated monthly shipments of brand-new books from your selected series, always at a discount off the cover price! Plus you can cancel any time. So don't miss out, return your One Minute Survey today to get your Free books.

Pam Powers

"One Minute" Survey
GET YOUR FREE BOOKS AND A FREE GIFT!
✓ Complete this Survey ✓ Return this survey

1 Do you try to find time to read every day?
☐ YES ☐ NO

2 Do you prefer stories with happy endings?
☐ YES ☐ NO

3 Do you enjoy having books delivered to your home?
☐ YES ☐ NO

4 Do you share your favorite books with friends?
☐ YES ☐ NO

YES! I have completed the above "One Minute" Survey. Please send me m
Free Books and a Free Mystery Gift (worth over \$20 retail). I understand that I am
under no obligation to buy anything, as explained on the back of this card.

☐ **Harlequin Desire®**
225/326 CTI G2AF

☐ **Harlequin Presents® Larger-Print**
176/376 CTI G2AF

☐ **BOTH**
(225/326 & 176/376)
CTI G2AG

FIRST NAME

LAST NAME

ADDRESS

APT.#

CITY

STATE/PROV.

ZIP/POSTAL CODE

EMAIL ☐ Please check this box if you would like to receive newsletters and promotional emails from Harlequin Enterprises ULC and its affiliates. You can unsubscribe anytime.

HD/HP-1123-OM

◆ HARLEQUIN Reader Service —**Here's how it works:**

Accepting your 2 free books and free gift (gift valued at approximately $10.00 retail) places you under no obligation to buy anything. You may keep the books and gift and return the shipping statement marked "cancel." If you do not cancel, approximately one month later we'll send you more books from the series you have chosen, and bill you at our low, subscribers-only discount price. Harlequin Presents® Larger-Print books consist of 6 books each month and cost $6.80 each in the U.S. or $6.99 each in Canada, a savings of at least 6% off the cover price. Harlequin Desire® books consist of 3 books (2in1 editions) each month and cost just $7.83 each in the U.S. or $8.43 each in Canada, a savings of at least 12% off the cover price. It's quite a bargain! Shipping and handling is just 50¢ per book in the U.S. and $1.25 per book in Canada*. You may return any shipment at our expense and cancel at any time by contacting customer service — or you may continue to receive monthly shipments at our low, subscribers-only discount price plus shipping and handling.

from the heat, but that river of honey-blonde hair
and that perfect pouty mouth were unmistakeable
even though he couldn't see her eyes because she
wore sunglasses below a stylish beaded trilby hat.
She had spent hours in the Al Qattara Arts Centre, exploring the archaeological finds on display
there and participating in a pottery class.

His wife…and wasn't it strange how the moment he'd *left* her, he began to view her as his wife?
And his wife, it seemed, had no problems playing
the tourist. There she was, driving an SUV and
trying to climb dunes in the desert—far too dangerous, he had warned her security team, furious
they hadn't prevented that. She was also happily
getting friendly with Saluki hounds, having her
hands and feet painted with henna designs and
dressing up in traditional Arabic dress for a photographer. She was having a terrific time without
him and she was thoroughly enjoying herself. And
hadn't he planned those activities for her amusement? Hadn't he instructed a private tour operator
to satisfy her every wish?

As the week stretched on, inexplicably feeling
like the longest week of Ares's life, he saw snaps
of his wife kayaking in the Mangrove National
Park, sailing, snorkelling and scuba diving. She
was fearless and athletic and what her shapely
curves did for a modest black swimsuit should be

outlawed. He hadn't liked the idea that her protection team had seen her so lightly clad and he was ashamed of that obvious streak of sexual possessiveness, which he had never experienced before. But the acknowledgement that lingered longest with him? Not once did Alana do what any other woman he knew would have done in Abu Dhabi when furnished with a bottomless bank account. She didn't enter a single designer fashion or jewellery outlet.

In the course of the week, however, Alana had made her presence known in Abu Dhabi without ever mentioning to anyone that she was *his* wife. She had been very discreet yet word of her solitary presence at his villa had still leaked out onto the local grapevine. In London, Ares had received two approaches from Arabic businessmen offering to send their wives and daughters to his wife's aid to entertain her and offer their hospitality. That had made him gnash his teeth and he didn't know why. He had politely refused the offers. Was it because he had felt guilty that he wasn't there with her? Was it because she was clearly having a spectacularly good time without him? Whatever, he knew he would be relieved when she moved into Templegreen, and he no longer felt the need to constantly check up on her.

'Your bride is working out very well,' Edwin

Graves pontificated at the end of that week over a private business lunch. 'Apart from that initial hiccup with her health, she seems a perfect match to your requirements.'

'Yes,' Ares agreed between gritted teeth because he now knew that somewhere in that list of requirements, he had got something very badly wrong. Self-sufficient? Hadn't he wanted a wife with that quality? Why was it that a quality that Alana clearly had in spades was now an irritant?

Was it because Alana was too young, too beautiful and too sexy? Was it because she had tempted him beyond belief and he had fallen at the first fence and destroyed all appropriate boundaries? Or was it because he had said goodbye to his mistress of several years' standing as soon as he'd realised that Marina mysteriously no longer attracted him, and that had been quite a while before his wedding?

Ares was unsettled and restless for the first time in years and he hated it. He wanted his life back to normal. He wanted to stop thinking about sex all the time as well. His fake wife should have occupied only a tiny slice of his life, out of sight and out of mind as she should have been, yet instead she had hogged ninety per cent of his attention while she had been convalescing in Abu Dhabi.

* * *

Alana flipped the page in her sketchbook again. The robin outside the window had *moved*. Now she saw that, regardless, the lines weren't right and that her bird outline was too static to be realistic and that drawing anything sooner than draw Ares's sculpted features was not an effective escape from the dark thoughts that possessed her. Fizzing with frustration, she cast aside her sketch pad—regrettably full of incomplete charcoal drawings of Ares. She stood up and stretched, her slender figure lithe in the scarlet yoga pants and cropped top she wore, and honed by the gym activities and the running she had taken up since her arrival at Templegreen.

This was her new life, a life cocooned in luxury against a backdrop of grandeur far different from any she might have hoped would one day be hers. Templegreen was a Georgian mansion of extraordinary style and classic elegance. After her busy week of exploration in Abu Dhabi when she was bent on proving to Ares that his departure had meant nothing to her, she had arrived at his country house to be ushered into the palatial master bedroom like a queen and to dine every evening in solitary splendour in the grand dining room. Whatever, she was out of her depth and drowning. She was the lady of the house, who didn't know *how* to be the lady of the house. The housekeeper visited her at the start of each week with a selection of menus. The estate manager came to her to ask if she had any special requests.

And if there was any special request she could have made it would have been for company, because the one thing Alana had not foreseen was how alone she would feel pretending to be Ares's wife in a world that was so foreign to her, a world in which expense was unimportant and in which ease and idleness were taken for granted. She couldn't ride the horses in her husband's fancy stables. She had toyed with the idea of hiring a riding instructor but decided not to bother as her future was unlikely to include horses and the leisure time to ride them. There was no point getting too comfortable with a luxury lifestyle that was only temporary. Exercising, making use of the excellent gym facilities and the pool at Templegreen had seemed a sensible way to fill the empty hours.

Keeping relentlessly busy had also given her something else to focus on other than the fact that her period was late. She shivered, suddenly cold at that acknowledgement. After the way she had stopped her pill, it was hardly surprising that her menstrual cycle would be unsettled and she never had been regular, she reminded herself soothingly. If her cycle didn't kick in soon, she would do a

pregnancy test, indeed she already had one awaiting her in her bedroom. That she wasn't making
use of it immediately could be put down to her
determination not to frighten herself into a panic.
After all, she didn't want to risk a false result by
doing the test too soon.

Enzo, Skye and the children had visited for a
day soon after her arrival. Once again Alana had
had to resist the temptation of confiding in her
sister. If she was in a mess right now, it was her
own fault. Why would she stress Skye out with
her anxieties? That would be selfish and unfair
when she had made every decision that had put
her in her current predicament without asking for
her sister's advice.

The sound of a helicopter sent her over to a tall
window to peer out. Her shoulders hunched. She
knew that she was only looking because the estate
manager had mentioned that Ares only ever visited by helicopter and that he was overdue a visit.
It made her wonder if the many properties Ares
owned were only for investment as he didn't seem
to make much personal use of them. He ensured
his various homes were kept in order but rarely
went near them, it seemed. She had only picked up
such little titbits listening to the staff talk. When
the noise of the helicopter became louder rather
than receding she went rigid, craning her neck for

a better view, and she was just in time to see the unwieldy craft landing on the helipad.

Barely a split second later, a tall male vaulted out and she knew immediately that it was *him*. Only Ares moved with that feral, prowling, outrageously sexy grace, luxuriant silvery fair hair blowing in the breeze, broad shoulders squared, back straight as an arrow as he strode across the lawn, disdaining the path. Alana literally stopped breathing, smoothing down her exercise outfit and flushing in dismay and wishing that she had opted for something other than comfort when she had emerged from her early morning shower. At that thought, her chin came up at a mutinous angle. She was doing exactly what she had been paid to do, living in his home and keeping her head down. But wasn't she also supposed to be *behaving* like a wife? On that thought, Alana sped out through the French doors and raced across the immaculate lawn to greet him.

Ares didn't quite know what he had expected from Alana, but it had definitely not included Alana flinging herself at him in an enthusiastic welcome witnessed by all the household staff. He found himself with an armful of fragrant woman and she smelled of sunshine…and sex? No, no, that was his imagination, which was currently drowning in such base thoughts. Thoughts that ran on a continuous torturous loop inside his head.

'Relax, Ares,' Alana urged, soft and low, as the tension in his big powerful body thrummed into hers. 'It wouldn't look like much of a marriage if I didn't make a fuss of you when we've been apart for weeks.'

Ares had to admit that she had a point. Wasn't he visiting Templegreen for the same reason? And hadn't he decided in his usual cool, logical way to straighten things out between them? There would be no room for passion or temptation once he told her a little about his background. She was a bright girl. She would quickly realise that no woman would want a future with a male like him. It wouldn't hurt her feelings either, so, on his terms, that was a definite win-win when her co-operation was essential to his plans.

He eased her slowly down onto her own feet again, feeling the slight brush of her slender, curvy figure against his clothed length and hypersensitive to that awareness. Of the softness of her breasts, the brush of the slim thighs he had spread. *Theos*, he was hard as a rock. A long arm clamping to her spine, he walked her towards the house, his dark features rigid because he was determined to stay in control.

On the steps of the imposing entrance, his estate manager awaited him, only to be dismissed by him in a handful of words distinguished by a clipped-off, 'Later.'

'You should've let me know you were coming,' Alana murmured flatly, stiff as a walking stick below that controlling arm.

'It was a last-minute decision,' Ares admitted. 'I'll be gone again soon enough.'

A stark pang of disillusionment cut through Alana and she hated herself for being so vulnerable. Coping with rejection was much harder than she had ever realised. Doing it with dignity was even tougher. She wanted to shrug and walk away and yet she couldn't. That contract had deprived her of such face-saving displays. Behaving like a conventional wife with Ares was a huge challenge. She had no idea what Ares would do next. She had expected him to immediately take off with his estate manager, keen to escape her company, and he *hadn't*, which only confused her more.

'A light lunch *now* would be convenient,' he informed his housekeeper as he walked past.

'Did you give her advance warning of your visit?' Alana asked.

'No.'

'Don't you think that was inconsiderate?' she asked soft and low.

'No,' Ares answered without hesitation. 'I pay

my staff three hundred and sixty-five days of the year, but I am only here a handful of days in that year. Expecting the kitchen to provide a light lunch on short notice should be a doddle.'

Alana swallowed hard, taking his point as he strode into the long gracious drawing room and offered her a drink. Mindful of her concern that she might be pregnant and paling at the prospect of that challenge with a male like Ares, who took nothing for chance, she asked for an orange juice.

'Make yourself comfortable,' he advised, seemingly unaware that his very presence ensured that she could not relax.

Yet she still watched him while he poured the drinks. He was breathtakingly eye-catching in that instant, his carved, classic features illuminated by the sunlight flooding through the windows. He was exquisite, bronzed and extravagantly handsome in his perfection, every line of his lean, powerful body balanced and fluid and outlined by his designer tailoring. Heat simmered low in her body and she looked away again hurriedly.

Ares watched Alana from below black lashes that carefully cloaked his expression. *Theos*, he was burning up for the sweet release of her hot, tight body. There she was, minimally clad, lush breasts barely contained by a crop top, pointed nipples on view and then those pants, hiding nothing, not the bouncy full swell of her pert derrière or the faint but definable cleft of her sex.

The pulse at his groin was positively painful. Just looking at her roused the most primitive instincts and the most powerful memories but he was not planning to surrender to those urges again, he reminded himself fiercely. He was going to do what he should have done in the first place: explain to her why there could never be anything deeper between them. Possibly she didn't even need that explanation, possibly she had already moved on, labelling their brief encounter in Abu Dhabi a mistake just as he had. Surprisingly, that suspicion was not as welcome to him as he had believed it would be.

Alana carried her drink into the dining room, almost bemused to find two places set close together at the vast polished table where she normally sat in solitary state. 'Why do you have this house when you hardly use it?' she asked as he strode up to join her.

'I used it as a conference centre before I bought the London house.'

'You should use it for relaxing at weekends,' Alana told him.

Ares collided with misty green eyes, reading the softness there and retreating from it in haste because it made him uncomfortable. He was very still while plates were slid in front of them and then he lifted his bright head and said wryly, 'I don't really do weekends or relaxation.'

'That's not healthy,' she pronounced, embarking on the colourful chicken salad with its tangy dressing. 'You need downtime like everyone else.'

Ares sipped his wine and set the glass back down again with the hint of a crack. 'You asked me a question that I chose not to answer in Abu Dhabi. You asked me *why* I thought we were a bad combination.'

Alana stiffened defensively. 'Those weren't the words I used.'

Ares lifted and dropped a broad shoulder in dismissal of that protest. 'What I meant was that I couldn't offer you what you would want and expect,' he intoned flatly. 'I don't do attachments. I'm not from a normal background.'

Alana's chin came up. 'I don't think that sort of a thing matters.'

'Let me try to explain. My father impregnated my mother when she was only eighteen. He didn't support her and she ended up on the streets. She was a drug addict and eventually she moved into a brothel,' he explained grimly. 'I spent my formative years in a cathouse. My mother abandoned me there when I was four. She took off with one of her customers and I never saw her again because she died a few years later in a car crash. Her co-workers in the house looked after me for six years until the authorities learned of my existence and intervened…'

Alana stared back at him, unable to hide her shock at those impassive revelations. He had spent his early years in a place where women, including his mother, sold sex to survive? His mother had then deserted him? She was appalled and she lost colour, her tummy giving a queasy lurch at the image of any child being subjected to the damage of such an environment.

'As a result of that background, sex for me is a transactional exchange bereft of finer feelings… and it could never be anything else.'

'You mean…' Alana hesitated in confusion. 'You mean, you…you go to hookers for—?'

Ares shot her a dark look. 'Never!' he rebutted with a fierce frown. 'I would never choose to *be* with a sex worker. I saw too much of that lifestyle growing up and I would never take advantage of such women. But in recent years I did choose to keep a mistress solely for sex. She would fly out and join me wherever I was when I wanted her and in return I supported her financially. It was a discreet arrangement and caused nobody any harm. There is, however, no current mistress in my life.'

A combustible surge of reaction overtook

Alana. She was relieved that there was no other woman in his bed but saddened by the dispassionate choices he had made. 'That seems a very cold, emotionless way to live.'

'It was practical. It would not be practical for me to be with you. I can't give you what you would want from me—'

'You don't know what I want,' Alana whispered shakily. 'Maybe I simply want to *be* with you.'

'A romantic wish I have no doubt died the moment I told you about my disgustingly sordid background,' Ares assumed with a sort of grim satisfaction that chilled her.

'No...' Alana framed slowly. 'Your background has no influence at all on how I feel about you. I am sad and hurt on your behalf that you should have endured such a terrible childhood, but it doesn't change anything for me. You rose above all that and became who you are today. That is even more impressive after such a humble and challenging start in life.'

Colliding with the surprisingly shining eyes now locked to him, Ares flinched and thrust his empty plate away to spring upright. 'You can't mean that—'

Alana stood up as well, pretty colour flooding her cheeks. 'I meant every word of it. I don't look at the world through rose-tinted glasses, Ares. But

I do try not to judge other people because I'm not perfect either and neither is my background or my parentage.'

Ares drew close, staring down at her with intent black-as-night eyes that glittered. 'You're full of idealism and I'm trying not to hurt you.'

'Let me worry about me being hurt,' she advised breathlessly.

'Without heels, you're too small to talk to standing up,' Ares censured, startling her as he planted big hands to her hips and lifted her up to set her on the table, nudging her knees apart to stand between her thighs.

Her breath feathered in her throat, her entire body suddenly on alert at the intimacy of his stance. The intangible scent of him that close stole into her nostrils, warm and masculine and unbearably familiar, starting up a sensual hum between her legs and a terrifying craving.

Looking into those bright eyes, Ares ran a knuckle lightly across her delicate collarbone. He saw the pulse flickering like crazy there and it lit a roaring fire of desire inside him that he could not suppress.

'Go upstairs and wait for me in the master bedroom,' he murmured huskily as he lifted her carefully back off the table again.

So, she didn't care about his humble beginnings.

She wasn't thinking it through though, still wasn't seeing him for what he was. But just how far was he supposed to go in keeping her at a safe distance? He wanted her, she wanted him, so far, so simple, only a male of his ilk knew it wouldn't be that simple. Even so, with his zip biting into his erection, Ares was in no mood to waste time quibbling. He wasn't her knight on a white charger and he never would be, and sooner or later she would wake up and realise that she could have so much more with another man. Unfortunately, the thought of Alana with the younger, more idealistic male who would be a better fit for her made Ares grit his teeth together in sudden rage.

Her cheeks red as fire, Alana glanced up at him, uncertain, charmingly disconcerted and still so innocent. And *his*. His *for the moment*, Ares qualified, satisfied with that amendment. The prospect of having Alana under him again momentarily struck him as all the Christmases he had never benefited from coming at once, turning his head with crazy glitz, potential and anticipation. He would reconsider the contract, have it adjusted to reflect their new agreement, but the instant that idea came to him, he discarded it again. For once, he would keep the lawyers out of it, run that risk and accept that self-indulgence always came with a price. And there was nothing more self-indulgent than Alana in his bed for the foreseeable future.

Encountering a burning glance from eyes that shimmered like gold ingots, Alana only hesitated for a split second before turning on her heel and leaving the room. *Wait for me in the bedroom?* That was so hot that it made her feel flushed all over and breathless. Why had nobody ever warned her that the desire for sex could reduce her to a mindless puddle of longing?

She walked upstairs. He had tried to push her away again by telling her a little bit of the ugly truth he hid from the world. But she had told the truth back. She didn't care what he came from, who his parents had been, how he had spent his early years or even his later ones. But she wouldn't tell him that *his* truth had almost made her cry with hurt on his behalf or that she was keen to learn more to understand what had made him so wary of other people and emotion of any kind.

Ares wouldn't want to hear any of that. It would hurt his pride. He would interpret her interest as pity or crude curiosity. He wouldn't want to know that she was falling in love with him either because he wasn't ready to offer love back. And maybe he never would be, she acknowledged ruefully. She had to be realistic too. In the bedroom, she peeled off her pants and crop top and walked into the bathroom. Heavens, she looked a mess, hair in a tangle, not even a scrap of make-up. He had to be sex-starved to still want her when she was so un-adorned. And maybe he was, she considered, when there was no mistress in his life. All she had to do now was persuade him that a wife could be a lot more entertaining.

And she wouldn't achieve that goal by telling him now that she suspected that she could be pregnant. That would be a step too far at this early stage of their relationship. That would shock Ares, make him batten down the hatches as he saw the threat of serious complications cloud his horizon. No, she didn't want Ares to feel pushed into what he didn't want, so she would stay quiet for now and not forewarn him, let their relationship develop without that limitation.

Ares strode into the bedroom and wondered where he would sleep that night. He would use the room next door, he decided, his intent gaze welded to the slight bump Alana made in the big bed. He liked that she was there already, that for once she had done exactly as he asked, that she had grasped that he wasn't in the mood for any kind of game. He stripped off his jacket, wrenched loose his tie, kicked off his shoes. He had never undressed at such speed, never wanted any woman with the fierce hunger that she inspired. And for once, he wasn't overthinking his reactions. He was going with the flow, no matter how much that went against his nature.

Ares wrenched the sheet back and slid in beside her, stark naked, bronzed and muscular and hugely aroused. When he simply grabbed her, Alana crumpled into helpless giggles.

'What's so funny?' he demanded.

'You missed me?' she teased.

'Yes, I missed *this*. I only had you once and it wasn't enough, could never be enough,' he husked against the ripe promise of her soft lips. 'I hope you're ready to spend the rest of the day in bed.'

'My...you've got that much stamina?'

'Try me,' Ares challenged.

'Oh, I intend to,' Alana confirmed, wriggling out from under him to push him back against the pillows. 'And there's to be none of that growly "you're a virgin and I'm in charge" stuff this time. This is my show this afternoon.'

Wildly disconcerted, Ares looked up at her with a frown, thickly lashed dark eyes narrowing. Her golden hair was tumbled round her slight shoulders and her green eyes danced with mischief and warmth. In a sudden movement, he kicked back the duvet and lay back again, his big powerful body relaxed and yet tense with arousal. 'Make yourself at home,' he urged thickly.

'Tell me anything you don't like. Can I tie you up?'

'No…well, at least not this time,' Ares breathed in a driven undertone, not wishing to squash her aspirations even though he could never ever see himself agreeing to trust anyone to that extent. 'Would you let me tie you up?'

Alana grinned. 'I think that could be something I might like to explore eventually,' she confided, small hands spreading to glance up over his ribs, a possessive vibe lancing through her as his hips surged, telling her exactly what he wanted. 'There's a lot I'd like to try, if you think you'd be up for it—'

'I'd be up for it,' Ares growled as strands of blonde hair trailed enticingly across his powerful hair-roughened thighs. 'Experiment all you like.'

'You're not going to get bored,' Alana promised, exploring warm little fingers stroking, shaping, making his flat stomach contract, sending an unmistakeable shiver through his big body. 'But you're not allowed to interfere unless I do something you don't like…'

And then she proceeded to tease and torment with a confident sensuality that was totally unexpected. It was the most erotic experience of Ares's life.

CHAPTER SEVEN

'WELL, THAT'S THAT COVERED,' Alana pronounced as the last slivers of satisfaction pulsed through Ares.

His ridiculously long sooty lashes lifted. 'Is there a checkbox you have to tick?'

She grinned. 'There could be, but that's for me to know and you to wonder.'

Ares reached up and dragged her down to him. 'Now it's my turn,' he told her thickly. 'And I may have a checklist too…'

He flipped her over and claimed her reddened lips in a passionate kiss, revelling in the responsive rise of her slender body below his. He shaped her straining nipples and a little whimper of sound escaped her. His tousled silvery head came up. 'Too delicate?'

'It's near that time of the month,' she muttered. 'They're always more sensitive.'

And it was true, perfectly true, she reminded herself, because her breasts were often swollen and tender coming up to a period. That there could be another explanation this time was her business until she had done that pregnancy test and she was determined not to do it too soon and risk a false result. A few days and then she would know one way or another.

'I'll be gentle,' Ares promised, dropping his mouth to the distended pink bud with less haste and more care and dallying there until little quivers were shaking her and she was arching up to him, having discovered that that same tenderness could also translate into greater arousal. 'We need to consider contraception,' he continued. 'I'll take precautions.'

That information lightened Alana's worry. If he was that careful, it was unlikely he had been irresponsible in Abu Dhabi, she reasoned. Just because she hadn't noticed him using anything didn't mean he hadn't, because she had been too caught up in the thrill of the experience to be observant. In fact, it challenged her to believe that Ares could be careless in such a field and most probably she was worrying about nothing. If only she had asked him at the time…but if she were to ask him now, he would surely guess *why* she was asking.

A blunt forefinger scored a flushed cheekbone. Brilliant dark eyes held hers fast. 'You're a hundred miles away in your head,' he complained.

Alana was taken aback that he was sufficiently attuned to her to have noticed that she had withdrawn. 'You're like that most of the time—'

'But not with you,' Ares contradicted, lowering his head to run his stubbled jaw over the soft, smooth slope of her breasts.

That roughened sensation made her shiver and he smiled down at her with sudden brilliance and then he kissed her, gathering her back into the heat of him, making her aware of every hard line of his long muscular body. His big hands roamed over her with the assurance that accompanied everything he did, and she could feel the heat rising between her thighs as he tugged at her swollen nipples and gently traced circles round her clitoris. A finger slid between her slick folds, teased at her entrance before delving inside her and she squirmed back into him, helpless in the grip of that flood of sensation.

'You're so tight and wet.' He savoured the words, pulling back from her and reaching for something.

He tore it open with his teeth, angled back his hips and deftly donned the condom before flipping her over, laughing at her gasp of surprise as he arranged her on her knees and straight away plunged into her, stretching her tight depths without hesitation.

'My goodness,' she burbled, eyes wide at the new tidal wave of sensation as her body initially struggled to adapt to take him.

'My ambition is to make you say a rude word. You never ever curse.' Ares pulled out of her before driving back into her yielding sheath with greater force. 'It's cute but unsustainable.'

'Not up to a conversation right now,' Alana wheezed, all concentration banished, her body now awash with the surge of sexual reaction. Dangerous little eddies of breathtaking need were gathering low in her belly with the sensual friction of his invasion.

Ares rearranged her with firm hands and angled deeper into her, speeding up as breathy little sounds started to escape her. Excitement grabbed her in a blinding rush, her body jolting to the pounding thrust of his until she felt insanely out of control. Her heart sprinted inside her chest—thump…thump…thump—as the torturous pleasure climbed and climbed and it became harder and harder to breathe through the sheer exhilaration of her response. The ache of hunger and need was unbearable until finally a starburst of heat flared at her core and radiated out in shock waves of drowning pleasure.

Breathing hoarsely, Ares watched her collapse down on the bed like a puppet with its strings cut.

He laughed, turned her over, dark golden eyes running possessively over her hectically flushed face and the drowsiness etched there. 'Don't go to sleep. I'll want you again.'

'Stop being so bossy.'

'Stop being so lazy,' Ares quipped, sliding an arm beneath her and lifting her.

'What are you doing?'

'Taking you for a shower…a wake-up shower,' he extended, carrying her across the room and kicking the door of the en suite bathroom open.

Once the water was streaming, he walked her under it and began to wash her with a cloth. 'I'm beginning to feel like a doll,' Alana protested.

'*My* doll…*my* wife,' Ares countered with a quirk of his sensual mouth. 'But way too feisty to allow me to do anything you don't want.'

The cloth moved over her skin in gentle soapy sweeps. It was the first time that Ares had referred to her as his wife as though she were a real wife and she liked it, she liked it way too much. It was a huge shower and he sat her down on the bench and did a very creditable job of shampooing her hair. 'Now you'll smell like me as well,' he remarked.

'What is this?' she framed warily.

'The prelude to shower sex. I assumed you'd be keen to tick that box too,' he teased.

'I didn't think about it—'

'You don't need to think. I'm very inventive when I need to be. I'm in Switzerland next week. You can join me and the week after we'll be in Greece together,' he reminded her.

He was finally letting her into his life, Alana thought on a wave of intoxicating happiness. Shower sex suddenly seemed a very good idea, particularly when she had never seen Ares act so relaxed. She watched the water stream down over his well-developed pectoral and abdominal muscles and stroked her hand in the same direction, touching him, appreciating him. She looked up at him, connected with smouldering dark gold enticement and her heart hammered afresh and her mouth ran dry. He lifted her and took her lips with hungry urgency, long, drugging kisses that left her mindless. Before she had regained ground, Ares had her backed up against the wall and he was slamming into her again hard and fast, making her feel every inch of him, rocking her world with such ease that it left her breathless and moaning through another seething climax.

Ares slotted her into a giant towel and patted her dry, wrapped her hair in a smaller one and laid her down on the bed. 'Have a nap. I'll see Rothman, the estate manager, and get up to date with some other stuff and we'll dine when I'm free.'

Green eyes verdant as a forest glade opened

wide. 'Even my naps have to fit into your schedule now?'

'You said you wanted to be with me,' Ares reminded her bluntly.

'And it's all in or all out?'

'Pretty much,' he confirmed.

The moment he left the room she got up and went back into the shower to condition her hair because it would dry into a rat's nest without it. While she decided what to wear for dinner, she questioned the sudden shift in their relationship. Had she let herself down by admitting that she wanted to be with him? No, no, she refused to believe that. She had never been the kind of young woman who sat around waiting for anyone or anything and she had taken her future into her own hands to shape it. Why shouldn't she be upfront about her desire to be with him? That had cut through the shell of his reserve as nothing else could have done. She didn't know why or how her attitude had achieved that miracle, but she wasn't about to question it when it was so obvious that Ares wanted her too.

Of course, there was a chance that it was only sex for him, but given time she would see how much of his life he was willing to share with her. She wasn't about to quit at the first hurdle, she assured herself.

* * *

Ares rushed through his meeting with his estate manager and settled into work, immediately sidelining or delegating anything that wasn't urgent. In the midst of that exercise he found himself questioning that laid-back approach, which was so out of character for him. Why was he behaving in such an irresponsible way? Why couldn't he stop remembering Alana's breathy little moans of pleasure? Or the dreamy expression on her face post-orgasm in the shower? Why was he still reliving the raw excitement of having sex with her again? It was sex, it was simply sex, nothing more, nothing less, nothing he needed to stress about. He was allowed to step off the eternal grind of the business wheel and enjoy life occasionally, wasn't he? And that was what Alana was for him, he recognised reflectively, pure honest enjoyment.

Inevitably it would stop being enjoyable and he would get bored, but he would have to let her down lightly. Of course, possibly *she* would get bored first. He batted that idea back and forth in his brain and discovered that he didn't like that idea, that suspicion that in a very short time she might want to spread her wings and fly free without him. She was young, a lot younger than he was, he conceded grudgingly. The contract only tied her to him for a year at most, and by then he might well be glad to see her leave his life. In the short term, however, he would have to keep her amused, and never in his life before had Ares had to make an effort to hang onto a woman's interest.

Alana came down to dinner in a strappy scarlet dress that fell to just above her knees. The lacing at the bodice and the pale full swell above attracted Ares's gaze. 'You look outrageously sexy. When I see lacing, I want to unlace,' he breathed huskily.

Still a little shaky in the unfamiliarity of high heels, she sank down in the dining chair across from him.

Dinner was very much a special occasion, it seemed, because there were candles lit and evidently the chef had really pushed out the boat for Ares's benefit because there were several very tasty courses and Alana ate with appetite. Ares made light conversation and was rather more sociable than she had expected. Coffee was served in the drawing room in front of the log fire and it reminded her of their meeting at the Blackthorn Hotel.

'You're lonely here, aren't you?' Ares guessed, his sculpted lips compressing. 'You can invite your sister and family down here to stay any time you like.'

'Skye travels with Enzo whenever she can. She's rarely at a loose end.'

'Come here…' Ares invited, stretching out an expectant hand. It was an unplanned move because for a split second he had been on the very brink of suggesting that she join him in London. That such a thought had even occurred to him shook him inside out. He liked his own space. He had always liked his own space and he fiercely guarded his privacy. Next week she would be waiting for him in Geneva. Presumably he was capable of waiting a week? On the other hand, when his hunger was at such a height, having her available on the spot would pay dividends as well.

Alana went pink and slowly rose to her feet.

'Take off the shoes. You're not comfortable in them.'

With a sound of relief she kicked off the shoes and came to him barefoot. His hands clasped hers and he drew her down onto his lap. 'Relax,' he urged lazily, the faint accent in his husky tone sending a little shiver down her taut spine. 'You're a walking dream of a temptation in that dress, *moraki mou.*'

Alana tried to play it cool while his fingertips toyed with the lace bow and then gently tugged it loose. 'Ares—'

'Hush,' he said softly, tugging down the bodice

to bare her breasts and bending his head to capture the swollen crown of one peak between his lips, toying, teasing, so that her pulse raced and her head fell back, her lips parting on a helpless moan of compliance.

His other hand smoothed up a slender thigh and disappeared below the skirt of her dress, flirting with the lacy edge of her knickers and stroking across the taut silk between her legs to start a hum of deeper arousal low in her belly. He tapped a fingertip against her clitoris and her back arched and then he tugged away the silk to play with her hot, damp core. Within minutes she was helplessly engaged in muffling her cries against his jacket.

He tugged her head back into the shelter of his arm and rested back in his armchair with a wicked smile. 'I suppose this is what you call the honeymoon phase. Tell me if I'm being too demanding.'

'No…er…' Alana fell silent again, fighting to organise her confused thoughts. She hadn't known that she could hunger for someone the way she did for him, nor had she realised that it would be a constant hunger that was never quite sated.

Hours later, when Alana lay in an exhausted heap in her bed, Ares began to pull away to go to the room next door. He never ever slept with anyone. He never ever shared a bed. But Alana moved closer in her sleep and flung both an arm and a leg over him, as if even sleeping she could sense his restlessness. Almost groaning out loud, Ares rested his head back again. She was like a little wriggling octopus in bed, at least one limb cleaving to him at all times. He didn't want to wake her up. She deserved her rest when she had been more than generous in meeting his quite insatiable demands. He had never had sex that often in such a short space of time and he had never spent so much time with any woman.

Unhappily for him, he didn't wish to hurt her either and that was an unfamiliar new limit in his world that equally disconcerted him. After all, she would survive wounded feelings. But the need to return to his own normality triumphed when he wakened at five the next morning and he eased very, very slowly away from her snuggling body. He texted his driver, showered in the room next door, dressed and headed out to the airport to fly back to London. He would text Alana later and he would show his appreciation with some splendid gift. Emeralds to match her eyes or diamonds to reflect her sparkling personality? Why not both?

Within twenty-four hours, a magnificent necklace and drop earrings arrived for Alana at Templegreen. She studied the river of glittering diamonds and the big central emerald in wonderment and read the gift card that suggested that she might want to wear the jewellery set in Athens. In other words, the pressie hadn't arrived on such terms that she felt she could rationally refuse to accept it. It was reasonable for Ares to give her the kind of fancy jewellery that people would expect a billionaire's wife to be wearing at an exclusive charity ball. At best, it could be viewed as a prop for the wife role. At *worst*?

Well, the wages of sin and all that…

Doubtless he would be surprised if he realised that staying to have breakfast with her or even leaving a note would have been more welcome to her. Her pale face took on a painful flush when, the following day, a superb set of designer luggage arrived and, on the next, a diamond and platinum watch. In the luxury gift department Ares was keen to spoil her rotten. Encouraged by such gestures, she was soon counting the hours until her trip to Geneva.

She travelled by private jet and limousine in the utmost comfort and arrived at a penthouse apartment in an exclusive hotel. Ares didn't actually show up until it was too late to make the theatre trip he had promised her. His business negotiations had gone on later than he had assumed they would. Alana didn't complain. Hadn't she promised herself that she would give him a chance to

do stuff *his* way? She had sworn not to judge, not
to make demands.

Result?

Ares spent an hour on the phone after his final
appearance while his busy staff milled around him
and she sat in a corner like Cinderella all dressed
up with nowhere to go. She retired to bed. Five
minutes later, shorn of his phone, Ares dragged
her into the shower with him, wrecked her carefully straightened hair while enjoying a passionate bout of sex with her…and then someone came
knocking on the bedroom door and he retrieved
his phone and began chatting in a foreign language
again while he got dressed.

Alana? Alana ordered a meal from room service
and returned to bed. At some stage of the night
Ares joined her in that bed, explained the sudden
business crisis in unnecessary detail before expressing further apologies and soothing himself
and her with more spectacular sex.

But the last straw for even Alana's forgiving
nature?

That was when she woke up alone again and
registered that Ares had slept in the room next
door. While she ate her solitary breakfast in the
lounge, she pondered her predicament and blamed
herself for misunderstanding the rigid boundaries
of the neat little drawer Ares had now put her in.

He wasn't lifting his ban on relationships, he wasn't revising their marriage contract either, he was simply using her as a sexual outlet. Or maybe she was using him? No, it would have saved her pride to think that, but she knew that she had only flown to Geneva with the goal of achieving greater closeness to Ares and winning, if not his love, at least his respect and appreciation.

Instead she had met up with a guy who put business first and wouldn't even share a room with her, a guy who placed his privacy above her feelings. How had he imagined she would feel waking up alone after the disappointments of the evening before? Had he thought such shabby treatment was enough for her as long as he sent her expensive gifts in consolation? Was that why he had mentioned a trip to New York in two weeks and a return to Abu Dhabi the month afterwards? He was scheduling her into his calendar as a mistress within a marriage that was no marriage at all!

'You're leaving now...' Ares gathered, noting the luggage stacked by the door, sending his keen gaze circling back to where she stood in a turquoise coat teamed with turquoise suede-fringed cowboy boots, an outfit that was so Alana, it made him smile. He liked the weird way she often slotted a quirky note of individuality into her outfits.

He noticed, though, that her usual smile as bright as the sunshine was markedly absent.

Alana let her attention linger on him. Heavens, Ares was beautiful. Complex, frustrating, infuriatingly lacking in emotion and dynamite in bed. But also, indisputably beautiful with his classic bronzed features and stunning dark golden eyes.

'Yes, I'm leaving.' She conceded the obvious in a flat tone since her departure time had been as regimented as her arrival time and nothing whatsoever to do with her.

'I'll see you next week in Athens.' Ares frowned, now wondering what was wrong.

'Hold the sex, though,' Alana advised as the front door opened and her luggage was whisked out by efficient hands.

Ares elevated a level dark brow. 'Meaning?'

Alana moved closer to ensure that she was not overheard. 'You made me feel like a call girl last night,' she admitted starkly.

Ares froze as if he had heard a hurricane warning, his lean strong face snapping taut, and he caught her wrist between his fingers to prevent her from turning away again. 'What did I do?'

'What *didn't* you do?' Alana slung back bitterly. 'And I can't say that you didn't warn me, can I? But when you get out of a bed you're sharing with me to find another one in the middle of the night it's not acceptable and, what's more, it's hurtful—'

'Hurtful,' Ares repeated, shaken that that should be her main complaint about an evening that had been a car crash from start to finish. Not that they hadn't made the theatre, not that he had had hardly any time to spend with her. No, she was complaining that he hadn't spent the night in the same bed. Crazy woman!

As Alana tried to pull away, he caught her free hand in his as well to hold her there in front of him. 'I'm not used to sharing a bed,' he framed awkwardly.

'No, it's not that,' she whispered shakily. 'It's that you don't *want* to, it's that you can't face even that amount of closeness with me, it's another barrier you're determined to keep up to shut me out… yet when it comes to getting down and dirty, gosh, there's no holds barred with you!'

Ares almost laughed at that final comment, but he held it back because there was a glossy sheen to her bright eyes that he recognised as tears. No, she hadn't been joking when she utilised that word, 'hurtful'. 'I can change,' he heard himself say doggedly, even though he thought he couldn't.

'Maybe the contract is a safer bottom line for two people as different as we are,' Alana muttered shakily.

'I'm sorry,' he breathed unevenly, something clenching tight inside his chest as he watched her fighting back the tears and he felt very much to blame.

Five minutes with her and he felt fantastic, but it didn't seem to work the same way for her. He didn't know how to fix what he had broken either. He didn't know what to say to remedy the situation.

You made me feel like a call girl.

He had misjudged everything. He had assumed she would understand, overlook and pardon his workaholic ways because she was usually very accommodating. But then she had complained about his preference for sleeping elsewhere, he reminded himself grimly.

'And to give us both a completely clean page I will share my only secret with you to give you fair warning. I've been worrying for a while now that I could be pregnant after our first night together.' Alana lifted her chin in a decided challenge as she made that admission. 'And I'm going back to Templegreen to do a test.'

Pregnant! It was as if a field of too-bright lights lit up Ares's brain, stunning, blinding, preventing any kind of thought process. In short it was an overload. Very pale, he stared down at her in disbelief.

Alana flinched in the rushing silence of his

visibly aghast reaction. 'Even worse, as I'm sure you're aware, that development is not covered in that dreadful contract of yours.'

Ares then found himself staring into empty space. She had slid out of the door, taking advantage of his shock. Alana was pregnant? His brows knitted. He could see Alana with a baby, but he could definitely not see himself.

CHAPTER EIGHT

'I'VE BEEN ASKED to warn you that there will be a delay, Mrs Sarris,' the stewardess on Ares's private jet informed Alana as the jet sat on the tarmac.

Alana had a magazine open on her lap although she wasn't reading. In reality all she could still see was Ares's appalled reaction to the prospect of her being pregnant. He hadn't said a single word but maybe that had been the saving grace of her being on the very brink of departure. For better or for worse, she had warned him. She should have done the test at least a week earlier but she had wanted to meet him in Geneva first.

Why? How could she ever have been naïve enough to believe that having sex with Ares would miraculously lead to him attaching feelings to the sharing of that act? How stupid was that? Tears burned at the backs of her eyes, and she blinked them away angrily.

Quick steps sounded on the metal airstair and there was a chorus of greetings from the air crew. Her self-loathing session interrupted, Alana glanced up and her eyes widened in dismay on the disturbing sight of Ares striding down the aisle towards her. The jet was not delayed, she registered, the jet had merely been waiting for its owner's arrival. Ares had also changed since she last saw him. He wore a black designer suit, probably Armani or Brioni, the expensive cloth faithfully tailored to every inch of his big powerful body, a dark blue roll neck hugging his bronzed throat. No shirt and tie? She was surprised and unnerved when he sank down in the leather seat right opposite her and spread his muscular thighs, fine cloth pulling taut.

'I thought you were staying on here—'

Ares canted up a sleek ebony brow. 'After what you shared with me?'

Alana went pink. 'I only said that there was a risk of that development, not a certainty.'

'We'll have certainty very shortly after we land,' Ares declared. 'I've organised a doctor to do the test. Isn't that test a little overdue?'

Alana could feel her face getting as hot as a bonfire and guilt squirmed inside her. 'I wasn't in a hurry to find out,' she acknowledged between the clenched teeth of mortification.

'I am,' Ares admitted.

'A doctor isn't necessary. I have a simple test waiting at Templegreen,' she pointed out.

'A simple test that you could have used sooner,' Ares qualified crushingly.

'It's not your body, it's mine!' Alana shot back at him angrily. 'It's easy to be judgemental when it's not your life being potentially derailed. I was nervous, I was *scared*... OK?'

'OK.' Ares compressed his lips at that admission, feeling like a bully. He didn't think it was the moment either to point out that his life would also be derailed if she was carrying his child.

'And while you're sneering at me about taking too much time to do that test, does it occur to you that *you* are the one to have neglected contraception?' Alana hissed, her emotions all over the place and violently stirred up by his unnecessary comments.

'I assumed you were on the pill at the villa. But I'm aware that nothing other than celibacy is full proof.'

'I'm afraid not,' Alana confirmed in a curt, driven voice.

'It doesn't much matter how it happened if it's happened,' Ares remarked drily. 'Bestowing blame will not fix anything.'

'Oh, stop being so pedantic about it!' Alana

flared back at him, her temper rising in spite of her efforts to tamp it down.

'The likelihood of conception is—'

'Don't say another word,' Alana warned him furiously. 'We don't need some mathematical take on the probability right now!'

Ares breathed in slow and deep. How did he get across to her that she didn't need to think and behave like a terrified teenager facing single motherhood? Alana was his wife. Suddenly, it seemed, his *real* wife because only a genuine wife could be giving him a child, he reasoned hesitantly. Yes, she was upset, he conceded, but his own brain wasn't exactly functioning at its usual speed either.

It wasn't that *he* was upset. He didn't do messy emotions, he reminded himself. Of course, he wasn't upset. Possibly a little shocked, he conceded, but definitely not upset and it was presumably shock that had given him the irrational urge to simply drag her into his arms in an effort to provide comfort. Irrational, out-of-character, foolish behaviour that such a pointless act would have been.

'You should have shared your concern with me the moment you suspected the possibility,' Ares murmured in a tone of finality.

'That wouldn't have changed anything,' Alana pointed out defensively.

'No, however, you would not have been worrying about this alone and getting all worked up about it—'

'I'm not worked up!' Alana flared in furious rebuttal, putting her hands down to release her seat belt as the whine of the engines kicked higher and the jet proceeded to race down the runway.

Ares was up in a flash, big hands engulfing hers to secure the belt again. Alana felt as though she were about to explode with rage and she closed her eyes then, rested her head back and counted slowly to ten, praying for the seething emotions that were so close to the surface to simmer down again.

When she finally opened her eyes they were airborne and Ares was ordering coffee.

'Herbal tea for me,' she intervened stiffly, because she knew that some people avoided caffeine during pregnancy and she didn't want to risk anything.

'I'm excellent in crisis management,' Ares intoned softly.

Alana almost rolled her eyes at him. He was so clever but he just didn't *get* it. Her baby, if there was one, was not a crisis to be managed. Her baby would be a little part of her and a little part of him and she already felt hugely protective of that tiny potential being.

'And I'm very calm, which would appear to

be a useful skill in the present climate,' Ares remarked.

And that fast Alana wanted to hit him again.
She set her lips firmly together. She lifted her magazine and commenced staring blindly down at it
again while recalling how wild and passionate
Ares was in bed. How did she equate that passion
with the chilling detachment of the guy she was
currently dealing with? Of course, that was sex,
not the emotional relationship stuff that appeared
to terrify the life out of him. Yes, she understood
that he had had a ghastly early childhood and that
that had scarred him, but did that mean that he had
to regiment his entire life like some frightening
genius robot and feel absolutely no warmer thing
for anyone? Evidently to Ares, it *did* mean that,
she thought with a sudden flood of compassion
that infuriated her even more. Why was she feeling sorry for him? Was she truly insane?

Ares was relieved that it was such a short flight.
He didn't like Alana being silent and still. It made
him uncomfortable. It made him start wondering
what would make her happy and then it worried
him even more that he didn't know. And yet he was
trying, he really was *trying* to be what his brain
told him she needed. Supportive, strong, unself-
ish. Only as he handed her into the limo collect-

ing them in London to take them to the doctor he
had engaged, she was *still* silent.

The silence in the medical surgery was pro-
found. The middle-aged female consultant chatted
inconsequentially to the nurse and the ultrasound
technician since she could barely squeeze a word
from her new clients.

'There…you see,' she remarked, pointing to the
screen. 'Eight to nine weeks.'

Ares stared transfixed at the screen. It was a
tiny blip the size of an olive. That that tiny bunch
of cells could grow into an actual human being
within a few months struck him as a fact worthy of
wonder and fascination, but then he was primarily
a scientist and he wasn't sure that that take would
be welcome to the mother of his child.

Alana studied the screen with a trembling lower
lip. *Her baby!* Her poor, poor baby, with a man
who would never truly want him or her, who would
simply go through the motions of fatherhood in
a logical, dutiful way. Unnoticed, she shot him
an unhappy glance. Her eyes stung. She blinked
rapidly.

The consultant discussed the blood test that
could tell them the gender of their baby. Ares was
all on board for that and failed to even consult
Alana as to her preference. He took charge, the
way he did with everything, she reflected resent-

fully. It was her body, her baby, but the way he was behaving, you wouldn't have thought so. And there he was suddenly being a positive chatterbox with the consultant about the hormonal effects of pregnancy. Now he would begin treating her like a basket case. How dared he nod knowingly like that when the doctor mentioned the possibility of mood changes?

'Lunch is waiting for us back at the house,' Ares announced as she clambered back into the limo.

'It's a long drive,' Alana muttered.

'I was referring to my house here in London. I can hardly maroon you at Templegreen when you're pregnant. I hope I am more considerate than that.'

Alana could feel that mindless rage building inside her again and sensibly said nothing.

Ares gave up and switched his phone back on. Did she really resent the idea of having his baby that much? She would be a young mother. A lot of young women would not be pleased to find themselves pregnant at her age. Especially when she had only signed up in the first place for a brief fake marriage that had now become...*what*? He attempted to quantify what their relationship now was and failed. He was lost without that contract. There were no rules, no guidelines. But the contract had become a bad joke after he had broken it in Abu Dhabi and the baby was a consequence of that irrational act. Yet strangely enough he wasn't feeling remotely annoyed about that baby. Ashamed that he had lost control...*yes*. Ashamed that Alana, whom he should have looked after better, was clearly distressed...*yes*.

It felt like a hundred years to Alana since she had last stepped into Ares's palatial London house. She had been ill and newly married, she reminded herself. She had also been naïve and foolish and utterly mesmerised by the male by her side. That had been when she fell in love with him, she surmised, when he had demonstrated how amazingly caring he could be. A sniff escaped her and Ares flashed a glance at her from his shockingly beautiful dark eyes, a concerned glance. And it was that last proverbial straw all over again!

Ares saw the storm coming and he guided Alana into the vast drawing room and closed the door in his surprised housekeeper's face. 'What can I do?' he asked quietly. 'To make you feel better?'

'Nothing!' she wailed on the back of a sob.

He helped her out of her coat, urged her down into a comfortable armchair and hovered. 'There has to be something—'

'Tell me the truth.'

'About what?' Ares frowned.

'How you *really* feel about the baby!' She gasped. 'Because so far you have faked everything you have said and done and you haven't given me one honest reaction to this pregnancy of mine. I want the truth. I can *stand* the truth. I'm not a kid!'

Ares thought very hard. 'I don't really know how I feel yet. It's all too new and fresh. I never expected to have a child—'

Like a hare scenting a fox, Alana sat forward in her seat. 'And why's that?'

'I planned to never have one,' he admitted grimly. 'It was a decision I made many years ago—'

'But why?' she persisted.

'I think it was my idea of revenge…*not* to carry on the family name of Sarris, to let it die out with me,' he clarified tautly.

Revenge? Alana was shocked by that explanation. Ares, who on the surface seemed so calm and rational, had harboured so primitive and passionate a desire?

'And how do you feel now that we've managed to conceive a child?' she almost whispered.

Disconcertingly, Ares laughed with what appeared to be genuine amusement. 'That the revenge idea was a leftover piece of my adolescence and something I should have left behind me a long time ago. After all, it is a melodramatic concept and I am a logical man. Why would I let my ugly past control my entire future?'

'Yes,' she agreed, relieved by that concession, feeling calm again, not even understanding why she had almost lost her temper.

'I can adapt to new circumstances,' Ares commented with decided pride.

'Yes…' Alana smiled. 'And outside the boundaries of a legal contract.'

'We don't need one now, but without one we have no framework,' he added wryly.

'How do you feel about the baby?' she almost whispered.

'I'm still considering that. You're very impatient,' Ares censured as a knock sounded on the door and he turned his head to issue an invitation. 'That will be Edith offering us lunch.'

Lunch was an oasis of calm after the emotional storms of the morning. Ares chatted away about the latest app he was developing, not seeming to worry about the fact she only understood a tenth of what he was explaining. And then he surprised her right out of the blue by asking how she felt about her birth father, whom she had never met.

'I asked your sister when I called her while you were ill, but she didn't want to talk about him.'

'There's really nothing to talk about because we never knew him. Him and Mum were sixteen when she got pregnant. Her parents threw her out and his parents took her in and after Skye was born he managed to get Mum pregnant again...which was me.' Alana rolled her eyes. 'They were just teenagers with no sense. Ultimately, he went off to an oil rig to work and basically never bothered with Mum or us again. He didn't even help to support us. He wasn't interested, so why would I be interested in him?'

'I can understand that. My father...' Ares grimaced as he voiced the term. 'I suppose I should really call him a sperm donor. I sent him a letter when I was ten years old and went to his office in Athens in the hope of meeting him. He had me thrown out by security—'

Alana paled. 'Did he know you existed before the letter?'

'Yes. My mother approached him when she was pregnant and he denied any knowledge of her as well. He had a one-night stand with a college student and, I'm afraid, it came back to haunt him. If he had had anything to do with it, my existence would never have been acknowledged.'

'That's appalling,' she muttered, thinking in honest horror of the mother who had abandoned him and the father who had rejected him. It was another little piece of the jigsaw of early damage that Ares had suffered. 'I was only able to shake off my birth father's indifference because I had a loving, kind stepfather, who treated Skye and me as if we were his own daughters.'

'Hence your loyalty to him, but I still can't overlook that debt he lumbered you with,' Ares breathed harshly. 'That nasty little gangster he left you indebted to was an accident waiting to happen. Fortunately he's now in custody and he won't be trapping any other young woman the way he trapped you—'

'In...*custody*?'

'I used a private investigation firm and presented a file of evidence about his activities through my lawyer to the police. He's now awaiting trial for a number of offences,' he completed quietly.

'I never thought you would take the trouble to do anything like that,' Alana confided with warmth and admiration in her eyes. 'I'm really pleased you did though. I was very scared every time I went to make a payment to him because he was always dropping hints that there were *other* ways to pay.'

'That's how men of that ilk operate. Get you in debt, get you on drugs and then put you out on the street to sell like a product. It's what happened to my mother,' he imparted grimly. 'The charity benefit next week is in aid of the homeless, addicts and women like her.'

Alana was interested in the charity and would have liked to ask him more about his childhood but sensed from the tension etched in his lean, strong face that he had shared enough for one day.

Ares went off to work in his study and Alana was moving through the hall when the housekeeper intercepted her and offered her a tour of the house. Alana smiled, thinking of how much had changed between her and Ares and that she was now being recognised as his wife in his actual home in London, and that cheered her up a good deal.

The house was huge with three wings built round a courtyard with a very pretty central garden. The basement contained a pool and a sauna and a gym. Upstairs she walked into the master bedroom for the first time, enjoying the sight of her luggage being unpacked right next to Ares's, and she strolled through numerous bedrooms before Edith, the housekeeper, was called away to answer a query. Alana paused at a door at the foot of a corridor and, when she tried to open it, found it locked.

'What's in here?' she asked the older woman once she had returned to her side.

Edith dropped her gaze and became rather flustered. 'It's just another bedroom, Mrs Sarris,' she said with obvious embarrassment.

'Then why's it locked?' Alana enquired.

The housekeeper shrugged awkwardly. 'Oh, there's some stuff in there that hasn't been collected yet.'

Her brow furrowing, her curiosity huge, Alana decided to leave the matter there for the moment and continued the tour while knowing that, one way or another, she intended to get into that locked room. Ares had made it very clear to her that this was now her home.

Ares went out to a business dinner that evening and Alana ate alone, wondering if they had really made a fresh start or whether she was just looking on the bright side and kidding herself. He wasn't likely to change his routine and habits overnight, she scolded herself. Expecting too much too soon from him would be a recipe for disaster, but she could see that he was *trying* with the separate-bedroom issue now behind them.

Later that evening, she was just climbing into the vast emperor-sized bed when Ares appeared and began to undress before striding into the bathroom. She lay there listening to the shower running and when he reappeared, she said nothing even though her heart was pounding and her tummy was full of butterflies. The mattress moved a little as he got in and then doused the lights. He didn't speak, so she didn't either but every muscle in her slim body was taut with the expectation that he would reach for her. Only, he didn't. Maybe he thought she was asleep. Maybe he found pregnancy a turn-off. Maybe he was only trying to be caring. It was a long time before Alana slept.

Almost the instant she wakened she was propelled at speed into the bathroom to be ingloriously ill. She was relieved that Ares had already left the room, presumably to make one of his ridiculously early starts to the new day. Freshening up, she wondered if a poor night's rest and her nerves had contributed to her finally experiencing the nausea she had expected to feel sooner. She pulled on jeans, discovered they were already too tight for comfort and grimaced. By the time she got downstairs, Ares was long gone.

The pattern repeated all week. He left early, returned late, ate precisely two dinners with her and made inconsequential conversation. It made her feel like an invisible presence in his home. As for that shared bed? Zilch…*nada*. He wasn't touching her any longer either. As the days wore on, frustration currented through Alana like a live wire. Was it the baby she was now carrying? Was that a passion killer for him? Or was he merely playing a difficult situation the only way he felt he could? Or even, was Ares just bone-deep stubborn? There was no contract now. He had only ever wanted her on a temporary basis. Was keeping his distance how he expressed anger at feeling trapped? And why couldn't he just talk about how he felt and if he was incapable, why not let her sort it out?

'Are you annoyed with me?' Alana asked in the darkness of their bed the night before they were to fly to Athens for the charity benefit.

Ares froze. 'No. Why would you think that?'

'You avoid me—'

'I work long hours,' he contradicted.

'Because you want to, not because you *have* to.'

'Working hard is in my DNA.'

'Being avoided and deprived of sex is not in mine.'

The minute those frank words left her lips, Alana almost groaned in annoyance because she had not intended to be quite that blunt. No, she had started out planning to be subtle even though she wasn't sure that subtle would get her anywhere with Ares.

In the darkness, a sudden surprised grin of unholy amusement flashed over Ares's taut features as he lay with care on the far side of the huge bed. *'Deprived?'*

Alana sniffed. 'I'm sure I have marital rights too. How am I supposed to feel? You hand out such mixed messages. One minute you're pouncing on me as if you haven't had sex in months and the next I'm in the same bed and it's like I have a physical force field around me.'

Ares was smiling. 'I accept that that would be confusing. I didn't quite see it that way though. I know you haven't been well most days—'

'How do you know that?' Alana demanded, taken aback because she had believed she had successfully hidden her attacks of nausea from him.

'Edith mentioned it. You should have,' Ares added.

'It's no big deal. I'm pregnant. At this stage pregnant women sometimes throw up,' Alana told him breezily, not wishing to sound like a sick person, an invalid.

'You're going through a lot right now. I didn't want to make assumptions and I didn't know what you wanted—'

'You could have tried asking,' Alana pointed out with audible impatience.

'You make it sound so simple. It didn't feel that simple to me.'

'But that's because that's you. You make a four-course meal out of every potential problem even if there isn't one that I can see!' she complained with spirit.

Ares laughed out loud, wondering why he had never met anyone like Alana before, why no other woman had ever dared to challenge him with such fearless honesty. He rolled over the bed, across the boundary he had carefully respected, and closed both arms round her slight frame, pulling her close. He was as hot and hard as he had been every night sharing the same mattress. Even at a distance, scenting the lemony scent of her hair products, sensing her tiny movements only feet away and hearing her breathy little sounds, he had loathed the belief that he shouldn't touch her any more.

You made me feel like a call girl, she had told him in Geneva. That statement had hit him hard and chastened him.

'So, do I have marital rights?' Alana teased.

'Of course you do, but after what you said in Geneva—'

'Let's not get into that again. I was upset.' Alana shifted into a state of quivering anticipation as he disposed of her pyjamas and brought his sensual mouth down hungrily on hers, sending every pulse in her body racing. Her fingers slid into his hair, possessiveness licking through her like a river of lava rushing along her veins, lighting her up inside with white-hot energy.

She couldn't get enough of him and he didn't seem able to get enough of her. It had only been a week since they had last been intimate but it felt like one heck of a lot longer. They came together in a tempest of passion as he sank into her with a hungry growl and the pace was frantic, feverish and spectacularly sexy. She reached a peak fast and her climax drove his, plunging them both into hot pleasure and gasping satisfaction.

'I'm never going to move again,' Ares swore raggedly into her tumbled hair.

'That was incredible,' she framed a little smugly, hands smoothing over any part of him she could reach.

'It was…and now you have to sleep. You need your rest,' he reminded her.

'When you get bossy, I get irritated,' she warned him.

'Go to sleep, *moraki mou*. Tomorrow will be a long day.'

Alana drifted off in a blissful haze, everything right again in her world, and awakened to breakfast in bed without Ares, who would apparently meet her when he joined her flight in Paris.

Hours later, groomed within an inch of her life by the stylists who had arrived at her husband's penthouse apartment in Athens, she walked down a red carpet into a blinding blitz of flashing cameras with one hand daintily anchored on his arm and an overwhelming sensation of being out of her depth. Yet she knew she looked her very best. The extravagant emerald and diamond necklace was round her throat, an embellishment to the designer white beaded sleeveless gown that swept down to her toes, highlighting her curves but essentially showing nothing. Ares had chosen it on that shopping trip before their wedding and it looked amazing, she had to give him that. He had added to her sophisticated appearance with a diamond tiara that very evening.

'It belonged to my grandmother, Katarina Sarris,' Ares had imparted, intervening to direct the stylist to put her hair up and personally anchoring that glittering crown of flashing diamonds into her upswept hair. 'It's a shame that she's no longer alive to see my wife wearing it.'

And there had been an odd dark tone in his deep voice that persuaded her *not* to ask for an explanation just at that moment when they had an audience.

'Did your grandmother pass away recently?' she asked instead in the limo on the way to the benefit.

'Yes.'

'I'm sorry—'

'No need to be. I never met her.' Expressionless, Ares glanced down at her. 'Tomorrow, we'll be visiting the ancestral home of the Sarris family. I've never set foot there before either…something to look forward to—'

'Gosh, you're suddenly letting all these cats out of the bag when I least expect it,' Alana gasped, stretching up to whisper in his ear.

'No need for secrecy now,' Ares intoned with

quiet mockery. 'And it is *why* I married you, *moraki mou*.'

Shock shivered through Alana's taut frame as they were ushered through the glamorous cliques of bejewelled, designer-clad women and elegant men, every eye welded to them as they made their entrance and were shown to the top table. A welter of introductions followed and everyone stared her up and down, seething speculation in their every smile, sally and glance. Who was she? Where had she come from? Ares Sarris's *wife*? Her cheeks were flushed by the time they finally had the peace to sit down.

'Why did you tell me that now?'

'You'll have to mull over it before you confront me with it,' Ares retorted with amusement. 'I was surprised that you haven't demanded an answer sooner.'

Alana flushed to the roots of her hair and then paled, annoyed by his nonchalance. But he had hit the facts dead on target and she was ashamed that she had stopped asking questions. When had she become so involved in their fake marriage that she no longer worried about why he had needed a pretend wife in the first place?

'That's why I told you,' Ares advanced smoothly. 'Heading off a complication in advance.'

'You actually haven't explained—'

'This is neither the place nor the time.'

Grudgingly accepting that reality, Alana sat back in her seat to watch the famous celebrity currently treating the guests to her latest song. With a parade of such world-class acts to entertain them the evening went past at speed and by the time Alana drifted off to the cloakroom, she was no longer as tense.

Ares was teasing her. Sometimes he did that. Having noted her revealing omission, he had pointed it out. Did he realise that she had far from contractual feelings for him now? Had she exposed herself to that extent? It was perfectly possible, she acknowledged ruefully. She didn't hide anything. She didn't play hard to get either. Maybe he had already worked out that she was in love with him.

Emerging from the cloakroom into an alcove with a comfortable sofa, Alana sat down and dug into her tiny beaded purse to extract a lipstick.

'The Sarris bride?' an English voice queried from the bar nearby. 'She was so incredibly young and unsophisticated I couldn't believe my eyes. Has to be the last woman I would have paired with Ares Sarris!'

'Beautiful, though—'

'Still not his type. If it's true that he was cosy for years with Marina Vasileiou, the violinist, his renowned preference lies with older, sophisticated brunettes.'

'So, he married a youthful blonde and festooned her in jewels worth a king's ransom. Sadly, there's nothing new in a very wealthy man falling for a fresh pretty face,' her companion remarked cynically.

Marina, the violinist? Who was she? Alana's sensitive tummy turned over sickly. The former mistress he had briefly referred to?

Alana went searching on her phone and found pictures of a tall, gorgeous brunette in her thirties, all long black hair, classic features and endless legs. A famous soloist, who looked like a supermodel. She swallowed hard, deleted the search and rose from her seat to return to the function room, refusing to even look in the direction of the chattering women. She didn't listen to idle gossip, did she? And she wasn't about to question Ares either. She had more pride than that, she assured herself.

CHAPTER NINE

FIRST THING THE next morning, the London consultant contacted them with the results of the blood test. They were having a little girl, news that enthralled them both, with Ares even beginning to consider names, which Alana had told him was premature.

'So, this is where…?' Alana asked once they were arriving at the Sarris property, having left the penthouse with their luggage.

'Where I would've grown up had I been born legitimate,' Ares filled in as the limousine swept them up a long driveway screened by carefully tapered cypresses planted like sentinels to cast long thin shadows across the sun-baked gravel.

'And yet you've never been here before?' Alana checked uncertainly because, as yet, she really didn't know what Ares was about to unload on her. It was not as though he was likely to fill in the blanks beforehand.

'You know that my father wouldn't acknowl-edge me,' he reminded her flatly. 'After he turned me away from his office, the local priest went to his lawyers' office and told them about me instead. They ran DNA tests to confirm the blood in my veins because they accepted that if I belonged to the family line, that would have repercussions for the family trust. After long discussions with my father, they reached agreement that I would be sent at his expense to be educated at an English boarding school under a fake name to protect the Sarris reputation—'

'But illegitimate kids aren't as big a deal in to-day's world,' Alana argued in surprise. 'Why all the secrecy?'

'My parentage disgusted my father's family, particularly my grandmother. A mother who was a hooker?' Ares grimaced.

Alana's hand came down on top of his where it was braced tautly on the leather seat between them. 'Only a hooker because your father refused to step up and support her when she was preg-nant,' she reminded him fiercely. 'Don't let that embarrass you—'

'I don't,' he asserted.

But he did. Alana silently cursed the Sarris fam-ily roundly for forcing Ares into hiding as a child. Exiling him to a foreign country for his education, his Greek family had ensured that he was imbued with the conviction that he was something to be hidden and ashamed of. Abandoned by his mother and denied by his father. Her heart literally bled for what he had been forced to endure.

'I was a very bright child and fortunate to receive a first-class education,' Ares added almost argumentatively. 'The lawyers did their best for me.'

'But, essentially, you were an orphan,' Alana reflected. 'So where did you go at holiday times?'

'Supposedly, my uncle's, my father's brother. By that time my father had married and produced his first legitimate son and I was still very much the dirty secret. Naturally, my uncle and his family didn't want to be lumbered with me either. Why would they have?' Ares asked grimly. 'I was his brother's mistake, *not* his. I only went to my uncle's home once and he passed away from heart disease soon afterwards. After that, I went to friends' homes but sometimes I just stayed on at the school. That's when I learned to work so hard. I was determined to succeed in life so that nobody could ever treat me the way they did again.'

'Completely understandable,' Alana murmured as the limo drew to a stately halt outside a huge porticoed entrance. 'So how did you come to inherit when they wouldn't even let you visit this place?'

'A terrible tragedy. My father, his wife and my two half-brothers died in a plane crash several years back,' Ares volunteered harshly. 'And even though from that moment on my grandmother, Katarina Sarris, knew that I would inherit she still refused to meet me.'

'Even allowing for her grief, that was pure bitterness and bile,' Alana told him, enraged on his behalf. 'She must have been a very mean-minded woman. You were still her grandson even if she didn't approve of your background and you deserved a more generous response. Nobody should punish a child for the adults' irresponsibility.'

'Which is why *our* daughter will never suffer for one moment believing that she was unwanted,' Ares swore in a raw undertone as he closed his hand tautly over hers. 'That is *very* important to me.'

Alana's heart lifted high at that adamant assurance and no longer did she have to wonder at his unquestioning acceptance of their accidental conception. Ares was so determined to do everything differently for *their* child that she could only be filled with relief and hope for the future. Whipping round in her seat without the smallest hesitation, she reached for him and laced her fingers into his silvery blond hair and kissed him. Ares reached down and unclipped her belt to drag her straight into his lap. He ground her down on him with a muffled groan of desire, crushed her pink lips hungrily beneath his and let his tongue slide in for one urgent sweep before pulling back from her.

'Sex in the limo is sleazy,' he informed her.

'Never had it but could be convinced otherwise,' she mumbled shakily, all flustered and pink, and then she glanced out of the tinted window and saw the assembly of people awaiting their arrival on the steps of the substantial house. 'Who the heck are all those people?'

'Lawyers, domestic staff. A big moment. The last Sarris arrives,' Ares remarked drily.

'The only one with any courage or honour!' Alana quipped almost aggressively, so protective of him at that instant that she was almost in pain because of what he had suffered growing up: the cruelty, the humiliation, the shame. Sometimes Ares wound her up like a clock and she didn't know what to do with all the emotion he could send sloshing around inside her.

'When did you end up taking my side?' Ares asked with a wry smile.

'When I fell in love with you,' Alana told him bluntly without even thinking about that declaration, because she knew that he needed someone to believe in *him*, not his wealth, not his power, all the other much more important stuff that made him the guy he was. 'And no, you don't have to reciprocate—'

'Don't think I know how,' Ares slotted in gruffly, stunning dark golden eyes locked to her lovely heart-shaped face in sheer wonder at a creature so different from him that she might as well have been an alien being. 'You don't hide anything at all, do you?'

'Guess I walked into that one,' Alana conceded as she scrambled off his lap to vacate the car, dazed by what she had revealed and yet knowing deep down inside her somehow that Ares had needed that support from her. Arriving at the Sarris ancestral home as the new owner, finally acknowledged for who he was, *was* a very big deal for him.

Alana loved *him*. Ares was in shock as he swung out of the limo. Was she crazy? Didn't she know how damaged he was, how impossible it would be for him to be what she deserved in a man? And yet with that unequalled generosity of hers she had given him that pledge regardless of all his faults. She was giving him a level of trust that left him breathless and shaken.

They were ushered into a vast entrance hall like visiting royalty. Alana felt overpowered by the sheer grandeur of the building but stood tall for Ares's sake. The last thing he needed right then was a wife cringing by his side as if she didn't feel good enough for such fancy surroundings. In a library walled with old books, two older Greek men, the lawyers whom Ares was already clearly acquainted with, set out documents on a polished desk for his signature. It was a surprise to her when Ares urged her forward to add her signature to his. As a celebratory glass of champagne was proffered, Ares waved hers away on her behalf and requested something non-alcoholic.

An older man approached them in the hall just as Alana was about to ask why her signature had been required. 'This is Dmitri, head of Household Sarris,' Ares imparted. 'But we don't require the official tour. We'll explore on our own.'

Alana sipped her juice as Ares strode through another grand doorway and she followed with less assurance. She had never ever in her life entered a property built and furnished on such a magnificent scale. Everything she looked at seemed to be antique and the paintings on the walls were huge and imposing.

'Are these your ancestors?' she whispered.

'No, this is the classical collection of art which the family used to show off on very occasional open days to the public,' Ares told her. 'I've read everything written about this house. I could probably show you around it blindfolded.'

Alana had to blink rapidly in response to that

admission of knowledge about a property he had been forbidden to even visit. 'The family' he referred to had been *his* family, but of course they had deprived Ares of ever believing in that blood bond because they had refused to recognise his existence. Even the death of most of that family hadn't altered his mindset.

Did you attend your grandmother's funeral?' she whispered curiously.

'No. She left instructions making it clear that she did not want me to do so,' he told her.

'Nasty old shrew,' Alana mumbled, aghast that anyone could be that bitter about an illegitimate grandson even on their deathbed. 'So, why did I have to sign those documents?'

'My grandmother, Katarina, found a loophole. Ultimately, she couldn't stop me from inheriting this place because there is a legal trust that prevented her from doing so. When I was still a teenager I gave an interview boasting about how I would never marry, which was, indeed, my mindset for more years than I care to count,' Ares conceded in a wry undertone. 'So, Katarina played a blinder. In her will she passed it all on dutifully to me with three little extra words: *and his wife*. To claim my inheritance *without* a wife I would've been forced to prove my identity in an open courtroom and that would have dragged out all the dirty laundry. It could have been done. There was no way I could be denied what is mine by right of birth but I was reluctant to face that courtroom exposure.'

'Of course, you were,' Alana agreed, reaching for his hand, squeezing his fingers. 'It would have embarrassed you and why should you be embarrassed all over again after what you've already had to rise above?'

'That's pretty much how I felt about it as well,' Ares admitted, his wide sensual lips compressed into a flat line. 'So, that's why I was looking for a wife, who *wasn't* a wife—'

'And ended up with a wife, who *is* a wife…or *am I*?' Alana heard herself ask in sudden helpless dismay.

'I imagine the jury is still out on that one,' Ares countered with his usual innate caution, while wondering how the hell a guy was supposed to handle a woman who was so open and impulsive and just hung everything out there when, all his life, he had kept everything hidden and locked down until it was literally forced out of him. 'It's early days for us.'

So, what am I, then? Alana questioned herself anxiously.

A *trial* wife? A wife only until she had given birth? Was that the date that Ares was truly awaiting? Once their child was born, would he then be counting on a divorce? What else could she be expected to think after such a careful statement? Her heart sank to the level of her shoe soles.

Ares strode into the portrait gallery, a space optimised to show his ancestors, including his father.

'That has to be your dad,' Alana guessed, scanning the silvery blond male in the modern suit. 'You're better looking...he's got a weak chin. It figures, a guy who couldn't cope with hard reality—'

'Yes,' Ares conceded, struggling to respond in English, disconcerted by that blunt appraisal that fitted the man surprisingly well. A man who couldn't deal with an unexpected pregnancy or a little boy, of whom he was the father, a man set on denying the truth until the day he died. For the first time, it struck Ares that that sperm donor of his hadn't been much of a man at all. He had been a coward, a total wimp when decency demanded that he should step forward. It had taken the lawyers to remind his father that Ares could not be ignored, that it would be too dangerous to leave an heir to the Sarris trust uneducated and unpresentable.

He had been taught at boarding school how to speak, how to dress, how to behave in polite company. It had been shell shock of the strongest kind for a street kid brought up simply to worry about his next meal and survival. His IQ count had been his saviour, allowing him to fly in every subject while the less fortunate floundered. But he knew, indeed, he fully recognised that had he been less clever he would've failed and sunk like a stone in such a challenging environment where even the language and the culture were unfamiliar.

'It must've killed them,' Alana whispered, scanning the line of portraits. 'What did your half-brothers look like? Were they blond like you?'

'No, dark-haired like their mother.'

'So, it would have annoyed them even more that you were an almost exact copy of your father, of the family Sarris trait of that very fair hair and dark eyes.' Alana's tone was celebratory. 'They denied you, but you were so much a Sarris from birth—'

'Never thought of my colouring quite that way,' Ares admitted, once again taken aback, gazing down at her, so little and so cute and so very much herself even in the medieval Sarris palace of sophistication and dignity. Ironically, she was very much more comfortable than he was.

'Of course, you didn't. You would've been far too busy concentrating on all the negative aspects, never looking for the positive ones,' Alana condemned with conviction. 'You never ever look on the bright side, Ares—'

'Except when I'm with you,' Ares allowed tightly.

'Did you inherit money with this place?'

'Not a drachma. There wasn't much left of the Sarris wealth. They lived high, earned small and this house needs a lot of money spent on it and the upkeep is costly. What little money there was after Katarina's death went to charity.'

'Such idiots to ignore you when you could have saved them all as a money-maker,' Alana pronounced with huge satisfaction. 'You were exactly what this family needed when their fortunes were on the wane, but they were too snobby and precious to recognise your worth as a tycoon. You were well rid of the lot of them.'

'How do you make that out?' Ares demanded, shocked by such a declaration when all his life all he had thought about was his rejection, his humiliation, the knowledge that he was only an embarrassment to his late father and family.

Alana viewed him in surprise. 'Well, if they'd been friendly, they'd have hung on your sleeve for sure because they undoubtedly needed your money and drive. You had the brain and the get up and go which they clearly lacked. I don't know what your father was like in business but, I assume, nothing to write home about if your grandmother died without leaving much money. They probably resented you going from strength to strength while they fell by the wayside, *yesterday's news*,' she framed with emphatic satisfaction.

Before Ares even knew it, he had wrapped his arms around his wife and backed her up against a bare stretch of wall.

'What?' she said in astonishment.

'Sometimes you're the slow one,' Ares growled, ravishing her parted pink lips without further ado.

'Ares…?'

'I never wanted you so bad as I do right now,' Artes hissed, wrenching up her elegant narrow sheath dress with a ruthlessness that led to the sound of ripping fabric, because it had surely not been designed with the possibility of receiving such brutal treatment.

'Is that so?' Alana couldn't have cared less had he stripped her naked because her heart was racing and her whole skin surface was tingling with sensual awareness.

Ares had that molten golden glow in his gaze and it melted her from inside out like heated honey. He was a very sexual male with a high libido, her perfect match. She liked to be wanted, she *needed* to be wanted when it was the guy she loved. It might be the lowest common aspect of a relationship but she would settle for what she could get while she built on other things. No, she didn't expect everything offered upfront like some women, yes, she was willing to work for a stronger bond.

Everything she wore below the dress was ripped, shredded, cast aside. Ares in a certain mood blazed with passion. He kissed her breathless, his seething hunger setting her alight like a flame on dry straw. To be desired to that degree was an aphrodisiac. It fired her up like a blazing star flaming through the heavens. She was yanking at that silvery hair, hauling at his shirt, clawing at his smoothly tailored shoulders, fully on board for every electrifying moment of that sexual connection.

Ares lifted her up against the wall and sank into her slick depths in one single, utterly thrilling moment and she shrieked his name in ecstasy as he stretched her to the limit. She needed him as much as he needed her and that was all right as far as she was concerned. Powerful pleasure consumed her from her pelvis up through her entire body as he pounded into her at a crazy rhythm. It was wild and exciting and she climaxed in a rush of sheer joy that wiped her out.

Swallowing a curse as the best sex of his life still rippled through his shuddering frame, Ares lifted up his wife and carried her into the nearest bedroom—that mental floor plan really did come in handy at that moment. He laid her with apologetic care down onto a gilded four-poster bed and studied the tatters of the dress he had ripped, wondering where the lingerie had gone. Recalling in a surge of X-rated imagery, he stalked back out to the portrait gallery to retrieve the evidence. His pregnant wife, and he had gone at her…like a rutting *animal*, he conceded in shock and shame, unable to explain that behaviour, appalled by it. There had been just that instant where everything inside him got to be too much and nothing would do him but he possessed her again.

'*Theos*… I am so *very* sorry,' Ares framed raggedly, staring down at her in shattered disquiet.

'Why are you saying sorry?' Alana looked up at him with tranquil green eyes bright as stars, blonde hair wildly tousled round her lovely face. 'That was absolutely freaking *amazing*!'

Ares stared down at his wife, his incredible sex fantasy of a wife, in wonderment. No, she was the amazing one. Every time he was with her, he was reminded of that fact, that she was totally unlike any other woman he had ever been with, and it blew him away. With her, he was the kind of mindless he had never been.

'But I've ruined your clothes,' he mumbled thickly.

'You said we were spending the night here,' she reminded him calmly. 'We bought luggage with us.'

Ares glanced around the room for the first time,

saw the cases as yet unpacked and let some of his extreme tension escape. They were in the master bedroom, double doors off the arch at the end of the portrait gallery, his brain reminded him once again of that all-important floor plan.

'I was rough…you're pregnant—'

'Still enjoying the passion,' Alana interposed. 'Not an invalid. Doctor said it was fine as long as I'm healthy and I am. Did you miss that statement?'

'Was probably still studying that screen with the baby blip,' Ares confided.

'Yeah, not much to see there yet.'

'But her heart is hitting one hundred and eighty beats a minute and her brain is functioning in the blip,' Ares informed her expansively. 'And the wrists, the elbows and the knees are forming. The legs and arms are longer too.'

'Right.' Alana nodded and smiled sunnily, relieved that he had relaxed enough again to be back to normal and telling her all the things that he knew and she didn't. He was also displaying a level of interest in their daughter's development that delighted her.

'It's really fascinating,' he confided, flopping back on the bed. 'I'm tired.'

'Course you are. This was a challenging day.' Alana sat up, tugged loose his tie, began to wrench him free of his jacket and unbutton his shirt and since she had sent a few of those buttons flying on the gallery that wasn't much of a task. 'And you gave me incredible sex on top of all that, so you've done astonishingly well, hit every Ares Sarris target, in fact.'

'Really?' Ares canted up an ebony brow, watching her take care of him as no woman had ever taken care of him and wondering how she could be so casual, so relaxed when what was happening to him felt so very visceral, so very *intense*.

Alana slid off the bed to finish stripping him, drowning in those glorious dark golden eyes like the addict she was. Shoes and socks went flying along with his tailored trousers. She wrenched back the fancy silk cover on the museum-quality bed and pushed him flat. 'Now you sleep. You need rest.'

'I just arrived!' Ares objected, flying upright again.

Alana pushed those big brown shoulders back down firmly again. 'You're knackered but you won't admit it. You didn't sleep last night. Don't think I didn't notice you up in the middle of the night working on that laptop! Anyway, we need to rest before we get up for dinner in this palace and act like we belong because we *do* belong here because this is *your* home now.'

Ares computed those plain facts, lay back and sighed. When it came to the ordinary things, she knew what she was talking about. She saw stuff in a different way from him, but it amazed him how good she could be in that line, how wonderfully, brilliantly practical.

As Ares fell asleep, his phone was buzzing. Alana scooped it up before it could wake him and the name flashed across the screen, *Marina*, and her stomach turned over sickly as she switched it off. His ex, his mistress? She didn't know, didn't really want to know after what she had heard about the lady, but she didn't like that she was still calling Ares after he had got married. Why were they still in touch with each other? Wasn't that suspicious?

Was wondering that even her business now? Where exactly did she stand with Ares? What did the marriage, which should have been wholly fake, now consist of? Her accidental pregnancy, she answered inwardly and cringed. That was no basis for a proper marriage. Her own intelligence warned her of that reality.

She hovered, just watching him sleep. Heavens, he was still her warrior angel, so unappreciated by those who should have loved and admired him for all that he had grown into as a man in spite of his tormented beginnings. And exquisite from that ruffled silvery hair to the long black lashes fanning his model high cheekbones and the perfect pink pout of those movie star lips of his.

He was hers now but for how long? Could she really expect to continue holding Ares's interest when it came to a temptation like that gorgeous sleek brunette she had seen online?

CHAPTER TEN

'PREGNANT?' ALANA'S SISTER Skye gasped as though it were the worst news she had ever heard, her eyes huge.

'Thought it might be heading that way,' Enzo remarked wryly. 'Reckon the way that business contract went off the rails so fast shocked the hell out of Ares!'

Alana frowned. 'How did you work that out?' she asked her brother-in-law.

'Know him, know you…it was obviously going to be a car crash—'

'Thanks,' Alana said tightly.

'A car crash in a *good* way,' Enzo rephrased with amusement. 'Never met a guy who needed to live a *real* life so badly. There he was inhabiting his billionaire safe bubble and then he met you. Not car-crash territory, I agree, but certainly a massive wake-up call. So, Ares is going to be a father.'

'He's quite…happy about that,' Alana said carefully, thinking of Ares's fascination with their daughter's development. A scientific experiment on Ares's terms? She inwardly shrank.

'He's accepted it, then,' Skye remarked, looking a little less panicked.

'Ares is amazingly adaptable,' Alana proclaimed with pride.

'Which he's basically *not*…in the slightest,' Enzo chipped in, unhelpfully. 'So, that means that he has to be crazy about you.'

'I don't think so,' Alana contended worriedly.

Her brother-in-law shrugged with elegance, all Italian cool. 'Well, what would I know?'

Her family had only been making a fleeting visit en route to a flight to Berlin but Alana was relieved to have seen her sister and told her a little more about her mystery marriage. Maybe eventually she would tell Skye everything but just then it had felt like much too soon to reveal the complexities of her relationship with Ares. Ares, the guy who only followed transactional rules in relationships, who hadn't ever been in love, she assumed. There was no straight path to reach a male of such intricate challenge. He knew she loved him. She thought he believed her, but he wasn't likely to ever say it back and she wasn't ever going to say those words again lest it make Ares feel trapped by expectations he could not fulfil. Nothing would chase him from her side faster or kill his desire for her quicker than that kind of unwelcome pressure.

In the short term, Alana preferred to keep her own counsel and concentrate on the positives in her world like Ares and her baby, rather than the disappointments. There was no such thing as perfect, neither in people nor situations, she told herself firmly, refusing to be cast down and constantly fretting about what she couldn't have.

One little secret, however, she did have the power to control, she reasoned with determination as she searched out Edith to request the key for that locked room. The London house was now *her* home. Hadn't Ares made that clear every time he got the chance? In fact, Ares was so fond of employing the word 'our' when it came to any kind of ownership of his vast pool of possessions that Alana sometimes laughed on that score. He had urged her to use his fabulous cars, throw out furniture she didn't like or find comfortable, redecorate wherever she liked. So, yes, she definitely had the right to see inside the mysterious locked room!

Once again, she noted the housekeeper's discomfiture but there was no hesitation about handing over the key. Edith did not, however, offer to accompany her, which once again persuaded Alana that the contents of that room were purely personal to Ares. And she had no plans to go rummaging through any of his private stuff without him, she reflected wryly, because she wasn't one of those women who refused to respect that a guy could have boundaries too. Whatever she discovered she would decide on her approach afterwards.

The first acknowledgement that struck Alana as she stepped over the threshold of that bedroom was that it was not a mere guest room, it was an overwhelmingly feminine room still littered with a woman's clutter. That knocked Alana straight off balance. Somehow she had been mentally prepared only to see an unfurnished room full of sealed boxes belonging to Ares. She was not at all prepared for what she actually found.

A woman's room?

Her disconcerted gaze locked to a large glossy photo of... *Marina*! And really, after that, there were no doubts to be had whatsoever as to who had once made use of the room. Alana's stricken gaze shifted to glamorous photo after photo of her husband's former lover. Marina in evening dress, Marina walking red carpets, Marina performing with her violin on stage. And the woman was gorgeous, there was absolutely no denying that fact. Overall, the room bore a closer resemblance to a shrine than a bedroom, she thought sickly, and she only anxiously tugged open one drawer on sets of daring wispy lingerie before retreating back to the door in shock, wondering what other intimate items might still be packed away and truly *not* wanting to know. She yanked the door shut, locked it again and walked away.

Curiosity killed the cat, she repeated inside her head, marvelling that it had not occurred to her sooner that the housekeeper might be embarrassed at her queries because she had assumed that no wife would wish to walk into such a room in her own home. So, why was it still all there in situ? Alana swallowed hard. Was Ares expecting Marina to come back into his life? Was he unable to quite make the break with Marina that he had insisted he had? Was it some sort of sexual obsession? Or was he now realising that he was fonder of the woman than he had ever appreciated?

Unhappily, Alana could fully imagine Ares being that blind to his own emotions and reactions. He lived very much in that world inside his own head, superb at developing technical stuff and solving business problems but barely more sophisticated than a toddler when it came to the more subtle, delicate promptings of his own feelings.

So, she told herself squarely, she was married to a guy who retained a bedroom for another woman. She could handle that. She could deal with that. Of course, she could, she told herself. After all, theirs wasn't and never had been and never would be a *normal* marriage and it was time she stopped pretending otherwise. Getting mushy and sentimental and wittering on about love was unlikely to solve the problem. But what *would*?

An hour later, Alana climbed into a limousine to go shopping. She had looked online but some stuff needed to be personally selected to fit and, what was more, she had been keen to seek out the most exclusive outlet possible. Heaven forbid that she wore anything on her body that might remind Ares of any other woman, never mind one particular glam, glossy giraffe-legged possibility. She had even gone back into that wretched room to check labels and she was ashamed of herself. How could she be so weak, so vulnerable that she changed herself to meet a man's apparent needs? She had never believed that she could ever be that sort of a woman and now she very much feared that she actually *was*!

In reality, aside from a couple of special occasions, like her wedding day, Alana was a white cotton granny-pants sort of girl under her clothing. She liked flexible and comfy and had not the smallest desire to climb into lacy bits of suggestive nothing or erotic corsets and suspenders.

But now it seemed obvious to her that that was the kind of stuff that Ares enjoyed and it would surely only be a very confident wife in a secure

marriage who chose to ignore that truth. Alana
was neither confident nor in a secure relationship.
She did, however, have a black credit card and she
wielded it like a secret weapon at her destination.
She would get over her discomfort at the prospect of packaging herself for a man, even for a
husband's benefit, she assured herself righteously,
emerging from the bathroom, barely recognisable
to her own gaze when she caught a glimpse in a
cheval mirror and swiftly looked away again.

Ares was due home and he was a guy with a
routine. He strode through the front door, went
straight upstairs for a shower and there he would
find her waiting. Simples, she told herself, no big
deal, just another step in the right direction for the
sake of their baby and the marriage she wanted to
last. Did she also need long black hair and perfect
features and legs as long as a rail track? Maybe
she was overreacting to that room. Was that possible? But she was always reading that men were
kind of basic when you got down to the bones of
them and there was certainly nothing more basic
than what she was doing, was there? Steeling herself, Alana arranged herself like a sex bomb—she
hoped—on the bed.

Ares came through the door wondering where
Alana was and found out. It was the nastiest surprise his bride had ever given him. He took one

stunned look at the outfit and hurriedly looked away again. It had never once occurred to him that she would get done up like that and think he would like it because she wasn't that sort of woman. And he liked that she wasn't that sort of woman, and catching a glimpse of her done up as though she were being filmed for some porn site shook him rigid. He lost colour, hovered and looked everywhere but at her.

'What's happened?' he asked, striving to understand what on earth could have prompted her into that sleazy seductress mode that ran so much against her character as he knew her.

Equally taken aback by the brooding silence, the tautness of his lean, darkly handsome features, Alana sat up in consternation. She hadn't been expecting him to start stripping where he stood because Ares was never that predictable, but she certainly hadn't expected him to treat her to one stricken appraisal and look away as if there was something rather indecent about her attire, because he was not prudish in bed.

'Nothing's happened,' she said defensively. 'I just thought that maybe you would…er…like—'

'No,' Ares sliced in. 'I *don't* like, *moraki mou.* I became far too used to seeing scantily clad women when I was a child. That sort of thing takes me back to times I would sooner forget.'

And that was the moment that Alana registered how crass she had been, to not even think of that possibility, that she was married to a male who had spent his early years in a highly sexualised environment and that such an outfit could be a kind of trigger for him. 'I'm really sorry,' she whispered shakily. 'But I wish you'd told me—'

'It never crossed my mind that *you*—'

'But it was all right when *she* did it, was it?' Alana gasped on the back of a choked sob of humiliation, because she was discovering that going out on a limb to try and make someone love and want her more could be a deeply wounding exercise and a mistake.

Disconcerted by that comeback, Ares quirked an uncomprehending brow at the identity of 'she' voiced with such venom. Alana kicked off the ridiculously high heels, snatched up a robe and, hugging it to her, vanished into the bathroom. The door slammed. The lock turned.

Ares breathed in slow and deep. Perhaps he should have mentioned that aversion sooner. Perhaps he should have kept quiet and faked pleasure even. He hadn't meant to hurt her feelings. She was sensitive, very sensitive, and she had clearly made a singularly weird but commendable attempt to be sexy for him. It was not her fault that he hadn't found it sexy. It was not her fault that he had frozen like a statue in the middle of their bedroom and found it too much of a challenge to even look at her. It was entirely *his* fault, because a *normal* guy would have been thrilled, turned on, delighted to discover a wife who made that much effort, particularly when she was pregnant and coping with all sorts of horrible side effects.

He knocked on the bathroom door. 'Alana!'

'Go away!' she wailed. 'I'm not speaking to you.'

'I'm sorry—'

'Not as sorry as I am!' she slammed back, studying her red face and anguished eyes in the vanity mirror. She had made a fool of herself. Rise above it, her brain instructed her firmly.

Alana stripped off the lingerie, peeled off the stockings, bundled it all into a heap and put the robe back on. She washed her carefully made-up face clean as well. Well, if he preferred ordinary, he might as well get ordinary in spades, she thought bitterly.

Barefoot, she emerged from the bathroom. 'You cut me off, made me feel stupid.'

'That wasn't my intention. I was just…shocked,' he finally selected.

'Wasn't really me, was it?' Alana muttered. 'I felt so fake—'

'It wasn't you. The last thing you are is fake,'

Ares asserted, trying to close an arm round her before finding that she had retreated several steps to make any such comfort impossible. 'I apologise for upsetting you—'

'It was that locked room that set me off!' Alana condemned.

'What locked room?'

'Don't be so dense. *Marina's room!*'

Ares frowned. 'I stopped seeing Marina long before we got married. Why would she have a room here now?'

Fed up with what she interpreted as deliberate masculine evasion, Alana closed a small hand over his and dragged him to the door. 'Ares!' she snapped when he proved resistant.

'You are behaving oddly,' he pointed out, and then he looked as if he wished he hadn't said that and, without further protest, he followed her down the long corridor to the very foot where she wielded the key and flung the door wide on Marina's lair.

'*Theos mou...*' Ares framed in seeming astonishment. 'She did like her publicity photos, didn't she?'

'This is *your* house and this is *her* room, so presumably you've been in here before—'

'No, I haven't been. I said she could use a room for storage because she travels a lot and it suited me. We met up at hotels, not here. This is my home,' Ares stated quietly. 'But why hasn't she cleared all this stuff out?'

Satisfied that she was receiving explanations, Alana shrugged. 'Not my problem. Your house-keeper kept this room locked until I requested the key—'

'Maybe you were hoping to find the equivalent of Mr Rochester's mad wife locked in here,' Ares remarked with sudden inappropriate amusement.

'Marina was phoning you only a couple of days ago when we were in Athens.'

'Yes. I've blocked her now. She kept on phoning to chat.' Ares frowned. 'We never chatted before. Why would I want to now? But I'll tell Edith to box up her belongings and contact her to collect them.'

His dispassionate response made her turn to stare at him. Stunning dark golden eyes framed by black lashes met hers levelly. 'You don't care about her, do you?'

'That wasn't part of the package. I wish her well, of course,' he breathed in an ironic lie be-cause right then he was wishing he had never met Marina and never made her his mistress. Her very existence even in his past was causing waves in his marriage and distressing his pregnant wife. Alana's peace of mind was much more important to him.

'Why do I feel sorry for her now?' Alana mumbled. 'Just an hour ago I was hating her.'

'You're a very emotional individual. I'm not, but I do very much admire the way you just put everything out there,' Ares admitted, pushing himself to talk, recognising that he had had a narrow escape from a ghastly misunderstanding that had hurt and upset Alana. 'I should think Marina left her possessions here because she was hoping to reanimate things with me, but then I doubt if she even knows I've got married since I haven't announced our marriage the way I should've done.'

'You admire that about me?' Alana had already moved on from the topic of Marina, content to credit that the other woman was a mere shadow from Ares's past and not likely to figure in the present in any guise. She understood the whole situation now, thanks to Ares's honesty. Edith had simply locked the room because Marina was an ex, who had yet to pick up her stuff.

Ares extended an arm warily and slowly closed it round her slight shoulders, greatly relieved when she didn't pull away. 'I admire a lot of things about you.'

'How come you've never mentioned that before?' Alana asked suspiciously.

'I don't talk much about stuff of that nature but I'm trying to change,' Ares admitted steadily. 'For you, I mean. Be less of an island, less solitary. I was thinking today that inviting Enzo and Skye and the children to visit us as a family rather than only seeing you would be a good idea.'

'Oh, yes, I would prefer that!' Alana carolled cheerfully. 'It always feels as if you're being left out—'

'Alana... I've spent many years deliberately excluding myself from everything *but* work. That has to change for your sake and for our daughter's,' he intoned calmly.

Alana was bewildered by that declaration. 'When did you decide that?'

Ares compressed his sculpted lips. 'Well, I would very much like to say that I realised that the day I first met you, but it took a lot longer for me to work out what I *should* be doing...which turned out to be what I *wanted* to do, so it wasn't that big a stretch.'

'I'm not sure I understand what you're saying.'

'I'm less than proficient when it comes to expressing emotion, but I can learn!' Ares hastened to assure her. 'When you told me you loved me in Greece I didn't know what to say, which was wrong of me. I should've said how happy I was with that gift of yours, shouldn't I?'

'You think being loved was...is a gift?'

Ares urged her back into their bedroom. 'What

do you think? Nobody has ever loved me before. I'm not the world's most loveable male—'

'Yes, you are. You're *very* loveable,' Alana told him chokily.

'You're not allowed to cry when I tell you that I love you,' Ares warned her. 'It can't be the right reaction, surely?'

'You love me?' Alana fought to keep her voice level and not bounce round the room like a maniac in celebration and gratitude.

'Don't you know that? I thought you would have already worked that out for yourself and that you were telling me first to make me brave enough to say it back,' Ares contended in some surprise at such ignorance. 'I only realised when you told me that you were pregnant and I *liked* the idea. But I should've guessed in Athens because you were such a tower of strength there in that Sarris palace that I… I just adored you for that—'

'Did you?' Her voice was small but her heart was swelling like a dawn chorus inside her chest. 'I love you so much, Ares.'

'I don't know why though. That worries me. You're everything I'm not. Open and sunny and free and I love all that about you, but it only reminds me that I'm older and set in my ways and kind of boring beside a woman like you—'

Alana's hands framed his high cheekbones, green eyes alight. 'You are *not* boring—'

'Even when I'm droning on about algorithms?'

'You leave me behind sometimes, but I'm not bored,' she declared with confidence. 'You fascinate me. You did from the first. I fancied you something rotten from the minute I first saw you at the hotel. I know you didn't notice me then, but that's all right. You're not the type of guy who perves on lowly employees and I'm glad you're not. I thought you looked like a warrior angel.'

Ares dealt her a slashing, almost boyish grin. 'Oh, I picked up on that when you were ill and I was… I was mesmerised by you seeing me like that. All that emotion just shining out of you. You were so tempting and I tried really hard not to take advantage of you and then I *did*…and it was horrible walking away again after being with you. In fact, that week I left you alone in Abu Dhabi was one of the worst of my life,' he confided, serious again. 'I wanted so badly to still be with you but I thought it would be the wrong thing to do for you. You deserved more than I believed I could ever give you. You were so young and bright and full of life and I was scared I would dim that light of yours, because what did I have to offer aside from my wealth?'

Her eyes stung. 'I didn't understand that that's how you felt and thought.'

'But you still gave me your heart and wanted my baby and that was…that was amazingly generous of you,' Ares intoned huskily. 'You don't care about my background. You love me in spite of it. You forgive my mistakes. You even make excuses for me when I get stuff wrong—'

'Yes, you really do love me,' Alana concluded with a misty smile, holding back the tears lest they freak him out.

'Madly, fiercely, *for ever*,' Ares stressed. 'I need to know you're planning on staying married to me until the day I die because I'd go crazy without you in my life. I'm sorry I was clumsy when I saw you got up in that outfit you wore this evening. I didn't intend to hurt your feelings. I hate hurting you. I love it when you're happy. I love *making* you happy.'

'I'm never going to leave you…but you do know you'll now have to celebrate Christmas and Valentine's Day and all those sorts of occasions. I'm a sucker for all that sentimental stuff and I want a dog and maybe a cat too,' she warned him anxiously.

'I'll cope,' Ares assured her with a wide smile, his lean bronzed features more relaxed than she had ever seen. 'What I couldn't cope with is being without you. You're more important to me than anything else in this world.'

Alana could feel herself standing as tall as a skyscraper. He was hers and far more hers than she had ever dared to dream. She tugged at his tie and he got the message fast. Off came the business suit, the gold cufflinks, the shirt. He lifted her up and kissed her with hungry urgency, telling her how much loved her, how he couldn't wait for their daughter to arrive. Indeed, now that he was finally talking to her, he was talking too much and she hushed him, which made him laugh. They repossessed each other slowly, both feeling so much more than ever before and no longer hiding it.

'I love you, Ares,' she mumbled drowsily. 'Goodness, we never had dinner.'

'We'll go down and find something when we feel like getting up, and that won't be any time soon,' Ares forecast, holding her close, simply enjoying that moment of perfect peace with her in his arms, safe and secure and his. He labelled what he was feeling as happiness and felt that he was becoming an emotional man. Once he had believed that that was dangerous, but it no longer bothered him because all that truly mattered was that Alana be happy with him. And she was.

Five years later

Alana tucked her daughter, Clio, into bed in the Sarris home in Athens. Her little brother, Lykos, was still snug in his toddler bed at the age of two. Both children had inherited their father's silvery hair and their mother's green eyes. In spite of a father as driven to work and succeed as Ares, they were remarkably easy to handle, even of temper and relaxed. Ares claimed that that was his calm nature coming out in their genes, but Alana thought it was hers.

It was their fifth wedding anniversary, but it wasn't the same date as their original civil marriage. While Alana was still pregnant with Clio, Ares had suggested that they hold a blessings ceremony and that was now the date they honoured. The ceremony had taken place at the same hotel where Enzo and Skye had enjoyed their nuptials because that was, after all, where Ares and Alana had first properly met. In truth that blessings celebration had borne a closer resemblance to a second wedding in which Alana, finally, got to wear a bridal gown and her sisters and her triplet niece, Gianna, got to dress up as bridesmaids. Skye's boys, Luka and Gaetano, had been far too active at the age of three to be entrusted with the role of pageboys and Enzo and their nanny had spent much of the day trying to keep them in control.

That very same night, Ares had dragged Alana down to that lake front and done what he had admitted he had wanted to do that first night when she'd asked him to marry her. He had tugged her into a passionate clinch on the beach before racing them both at an indecent pace to their room to celebrate in privacy.

Those days of emotional and physical restraint that Ares had once imposed on himself were now far behind them, Alana reflected happily. Their children had taught Ares how to relax. Add in a rescue puppy called Loopy and a black tomcat called Misha and theirs had become a busy household. They spent most of the week in London and weekends in the country or visiting Skye and Enzo abroad.

Alana had chosen to finally tell her sister about her stepfather's gambling debts. She had told Enzo first to get his advice and he had reckoned that Skye had moved on enough from the past to handle the revelation that their stepfather had been imperfect. Sharing that secret had allowed the sisters to return to their close relationship and now it was Alana rather than Ares chatting on the phone late at night, to her sibling when their children were in bed.

The Sarris home was still a very grand property. Over time, Alana had also become a little grander. This evening, she wore a sleek red designer gown with diamonds at her throat. Earlier that day she had worn a very smart suit to give a short speech at Ares's charity foundation, which she was now involved with. Raising money for good causes kept her busy, well, that and ensuring that she and Ares spent little time apart. Once she had teased him about being possessive and now she didn't dare because the longer she was with him, the closer they became and the less tolerant she was of being without him.

Now, Alana strolled down the superb carved staircase to move out to the imposing terrace where their anniversary dinner was being served. Just the two of them, just as she preferred. Ares emerged from the house to join her, resplendent in a dinner jacket, and she studied him with pleasure. But there he was, still her warrior angel, who made her heart pound and her mouth run dry while a tiny little hum awakened low in her pelvis.

She walked towards him, and a flashing smile of tremendous warmth swept his lean, strong face. 'You look amazing in that dress,' he told her, linking both arms round her to draw her close.

She didn't tell him that he always looked amazing, because he got embarrassed when she mentioned his good looks. Instead, she quietly revelled in the knowledge that he was hers.

'You also make me amazingly happy, *moraki mou*,' Ares confided, reluctant to cloud the evening with the truth that he didn't think he had known what happiness was until he met her. Yes, they had had their ups and downs until he had learned how to appreciate the gift he had been given, but right now in the moment he knew that he was holding the woman who was the centre of his world.

'I love you,' she murmured, gazing up at him with her clear green eyes.

'We're dropping the children off with Enzo and Skye in Italy and spending a few days in Abu Dhabi.' Ares revealed his surprise gift.

'You're taking time off again?' Alana gasped.

'Again,' he emphasised with quiet pride in that sacrifice of working hours, because making Alana happy was always his goal.

Alana locked both arms round his neck in her enthusiasm. 'I love you ten times more than I did a minute ago!'

His sensual mouth claimed hers with hungry brevity and when she would have continued it, he closed a hand over hers to walk her back to the table and pull out a chair for her. 'You're the most wonderful woman I've ever met but you still need to eat to fuel your energy.'

A languorous gleam in her gaze, Alana dealt
him a smile of anticipation, sparks of excitement
dancing through her bloodstream like glitter.

As assured as ever, Ares sank down in his seat
and shook out his napkin. 'I love you, Alana Sarris. I love the children you've given me. You've
turned me inside out and upside down with emotion and I even love that.'

'I'm such a great influence,' Alana told him
irrepressibly.

* * * * *

Caught up in the drama of
The Maid's Pregnancy Bombshell?
*Then you're sure to fall for the first instalment in
the Cinderella Sisters for Billionaires duet*
The Maid Married to the Billionaire!

*And why not also try these other stories
by Lynne Graham?*

Promoted to the Greek's Wife
The Heirs His Housekeeper Carried
The King's Christmas Heir
The Italian's Bride Worth Billions
The Baby the Desert King Must Claim

Available now!

#4161 BOUND BY HER BABY REVELATION
Hot Winter Escapes
by Cathy Williams

Kaya's late mentor was like a second mother to her. So Kaya's astounded to learn she won't inherit her home—her mentor's secret son will. Tycoon Leo plans to sell the property and return to his world. But soon their impalpable desire leaves them forever bound by the consequence...

#4162 AN HEIR MADE IN HAWAII
Hot Winter Escapes
by Emmy Grayson

Nicholas Lassard never planned to be a father. But when business negotiations with Anika Pierce lead to his penthouse, she's left with bombshell news. He vows to give his child the upbringing he never had, but before that, he must admit that their connection runs far deeper than their passion...

#4163 CLAIMED BY THE CROWN PRINCE
Hot Winter Escapes
by Abby Green

Fleeing an arranged marriage to a king is easy for Princess Laia—remaining hidden is harder! When his brother, Crown Prince Dax, tracks her down, she strands them on a private island. Laia's unprepared for their chemistry, and ten days alone in paradise makes it impossible to avoid temptation!

#4164 ONE FORBIDDEN NIGHT IN PARADISE
Hot Winter Escapes
by Louise Fuller

House-sitting an idyllic beachside villa gives Jemima Friday the solitude she craves after a gut-wrenching betrayal. So when she runs into charismatic stranger Chase, their instant heat is a complication she doesn't need! Until they share a night of unrivaled pleasure on his lavish yacht, and it changes *everything*...

#4165 A NINE-MONTH DEAL WITH HER HUSBAND
Hot Winter Escapes
by Joss Wood
Millie Piper's on-paper marriage to CEO Benedikt Jónsson gave her ownership over her life and her billion-dollar inheritance. Now Millie wants a baby, so it's only right that she asks Ben for a divorce first. She doesn't expect her shocking attraction to her convenient husband! Dare she propose that *Ben* father her child?

#4166 SNOWBOUND WITH THE IRRESISTIBLE SICILIAN
Hot Winter Escapes
by Maya Blake
Shy Giada Parker can't believe she agreed to take her überconfident twin's place in securing work with ruthless Alessio Montaldi. Until a blizzard strands her in Alessio's opulent Swiss chalet and steeling her body against his magnetic gaze becomes Giada's hardest challenge yet!

#4167 UNDOING HIS INNOCENT ENEMY
Hot Winter Escapes
by Heidi Rice
Wildlife photographer Cara prizes her independence as the only way to avoid risky emotional entanglements. Until a storm traps her in reclusive billionaire Logan's luxurious lodge, and there's nowhere to hide from their sexual tension! Logan's everything Cara shouldn't want but he's all she craves...

#4168 IN BED WITH HER BILLIONAIRE BODYGUARD
Hot Winter Escapes
by Pippa Roscoe
Visiting an Austrian ski resort is the first step in Hope Harcourt's plan to take back her family's luxury empire. Having the gorgeous security magnate Luca Calvino follow her every move, protecting her from her unscrupulous rivals, isn't! Especially when their forbidden relationship begins to cross a line...

YOU CAN FIND MORE INFORMATION ON UPCOMING HARLEQUIN TITLES, FREE EXCERPTS AND MORE AT HARLEQUIN.COM.

HPCNMRB1123

HARLEQUIN
PLUS

Try the best multimedia subscription service for romance readers like you!

Read, Watch and Play.

Experience the easiest way to get the romance content you crave.

Start your **FREE TRIAL** at
<u>www.harlequinplus.com/freetrial</u>.